THE RESCUE OF
JOSH POWERS

Also by Timothy Peters

THE RESCUE OF JOSH POWERS

TIMOTHY PETERS

ABUNDANT HARVEST
PUBLISHING

The Rescue of Josh Powers
Copyright © 2019 by Timothy Peters

Editing/Formatting: Erik V. Sahakian
Cover Design/Layout/Photo: Andrew Enos

All Scripture is taken from the New King James Version of the
Bible. Copyright © 1979, 1980, 1982 by Thomas Nelson, Inc.
Used by permission. All rights reserved.

Library of Congress Control Number: 2018965515

ISBN 978-1-7327173-3-6
First Printing: February 2019

FOR INFORMATION CONTACT:

Abundant Harvest Publishing
35145 Oak Glen Rd
Yucaipa, CA 92399
www.abundantharvestpublishing.com

Printed in the United States of America

TABLE OF CONTENTS

For my daughter, Alisha, her husband, Nick, and their children, Brooke and Vance.

CHAPTER 1

"Oh no! Not again," said Joshua Powers. The fifteen-year-old pilot had lost another engine in his Piper PA-11. The engine froze and shook the whole plane. Josh pulled his headset off, opened the window, and looked around for a safe place to put the airplane down. The only thing he could see was the dark green jungle of what he thought was called Guatemala.

His eyes searched the jungle for a straight line that would indicate a road or trail. He looked over to the right, but the sun was too bright that he couldn't see anything. His eyes traced around the front of the airplane and there it was! Off to the left was a faint line cutting across the jungle. He only hoped he could make it there.

The plane was going down fast and this emergency runway didn't seem to get any closer. Josh knew if he didn't make it to the runway he would probably be killed in the dense, green jungle. He hadn't put out a "mayday" call because no one would hear it. The last time he crashed into a river, he knew where he was. This time he knew he was on a course to rescue a sick missionary child from an Indian village in the middle of Guatemala, but that was all. The Indian village was so remote it only had a small dirt runway. No telephone or anything, just a radio so the Anderson's could call other missionaries.

The Anderson's had called their neighbor, who repeated the message to three other missionaries until it got to Josh's mother in Belize. Doug Powers, Josh's dad, was away on another mission trip, so his mother asked him to go. He was glad to do it. He had been sitting around wanting something to do and this had seemed like the adventure he wanted—a real missionary aviation project. But now out over the jungle, with his engine out, he wished he had waited for his dad.

"Father, you know I need Your help to pull this off. Please help me fly this plane and make it to the road. Father, forgive my sins. You know I don't want to die, but have Your will with me, in Jesus' name, amen," Josh prayed out loud.

The airplane was still going down too fast. Josh pulled back on the stick and slowed it just above stall speed. When he was finally lined up with the old road, he released the back pressure and let the airplane fly. He didn't have the engine to correct a short landing, so he had to make the flight path last until he got to the end of the road.

The road or runway through the jungle didn't seem to go anywhere. It was a straight line across the brush and ended in the jungle. It was like someone had started to cut a road and then just stopped. Josh hoped it was at least smooth. He had to clear the thirty-foot trees at the end of this runway. If it were ten or twenty feet short, it would be the end. The jungle would shred him and his airplane.

The giant trees were coming up fast. If he could just hold the plane up until he cleared the last one, he knew he could get the plane down on the ground. He pulled back on the stick and the stall warning horn sounded. That sound always made his heart race. He let off the back pressure as the last tree hit the bottom of the airplane and tore open the fabric on the underside. The plane hit the tree so hard it skidded around in the air and Josh had to correct it before it hit the ground. When he got the plane corrected and pointed down toward the runway, he saw the brush and trees were about four feet tall. The jungle had started to reclaim this strip.

Josh didn't want to land in the tall brush, but he didn't have a choice. The crosswind was harder than he thought and the runway was more narrow. He grabbed the airplane into the wind and continued his descent. The wind kept blowing him off course and he fought to keep the plane going down the runway. Finally, when he was ten feet off the ground, he straightened the plane out and let it settle to the ground.

The brush was thicker than he had expected. It tore holes in the wings, snapped off, cracked and popped, and struck the windshield. A small sharp stick penetrated the plastic and shot over his shoulder into the back seat. Josh felt himself dodging the flying projectile, but kept his attention on the landing.

When the wheels finally hit the ground, the plane was going too fast. It rolled on the front wheels for a few feet until he felt the tail wheel hit the ground. At last, he was on the ground! He decided not to use the brakes and let the airplane roll to a stop.

Suddenly, the plane jerked abruptly to the left and skidded sideways. Josh stabbed his foot down on the right rudder peddle, trying to get the plane back under control. His head slammed into the window on the left side and broke a large hole in the plastic. The broken window cut his cheek and the bridge of his nose. Josh held on as the plane skidded and twisted sideways, and then came to a stop off the runway as it was covered by the trees. The dust from the crash filtered through the broken window and covered him and everything in the plane with a layer of dirt.

Josh sat staring at the trees that engulfed the front of the airplane. All around the cockpit were trees. The airplane had gone from a safe place to a crash land in the jungle. He reached up and flipped off the master switch and then the fuel selectors too.

When he looked out of the left side of the airplane he saw a tree the size of his arm poking up through the wing and aviation gas running down the trunk. That scared Josh. He reached over and tried to open the window on the top of the door. There wasn't enough room outside the plane for the window to swing up because of the trees and bushes—it could only open a few inches.

Josh reached down, unlatched the bottom of the door, and pushed it out. The door went down a level and stopped. He pushed as hard as he could to get the door to go down more, but that was as far as it would go. He looked at the escaping fuel again. There was more gas flowing down the tree as the rich smell of aviation fuel filled the cockpit.

"Father, You know that I need Your help to get out of this plane. I don't want to get burned alive. Please give me the wisdom to get out."

Josh pulled the door closed and looked out of the window to see what was stopping the door from opening. The tire of the plane had cleared everything out of the way except for two small sticks.

If he pushed the window out as far as it would go, there would be a slot between the window and door. The space was just big enough for him to get his arm through. He unbuckled his seatbelt, slid over to the window, and stuck his arm down through the opening. He grabbed the first small tree and yanked up on it. The tree came right out of the ground as he banged his elbow on the bottom of the window.

"Wow, that hurt," Josh moaned, as he dropped the tree on the ground.

Josh pulled his arm back in and rubbed his elbow. He sat and thought about what just happened.

The airplane must have hit something. I hope it is not too much damage.

He stuck his arm back out of the slot at the bottom of the window and got ahold of the second tree. Carefully, he pulled up. This one didn't budge. He tried again with a jerk. Still nothing. Josh wiggled the tree back and forth, trying to get it loose. Nothing!

Finally, he reached out as far as he could, bent it back underneath the plane, and stuck it in the fabric.

Josh reached up, unlatched the door, and let it fall down against the side of the plane. He knew he could get out, but he would have to crawl out without opening the top half of the door. He put his one leg up over the control stick and slid down under the dashboard of the plane the best he could. When he had done that, his head and shoulders were still above the bottom of the window.

He turned his body so he could wrap around the seat and get his head low enough to get out. He was glad no one was watching because this had to look ridiculous. When his head was low enough to get out of the plane, he turned and twisted and pushed with his feet. His head slid out of the plane and then his shoulder. Before he could get his arms out, he fell to the ground.

He landed on his back and knocked the air out of him. Josh rested there for a couple of minutes and then tried to stand up. When he looked at the plane, he couldn't believe how it badly it had been damaged. The plane was tilted to the left with the right wing high in the trees. Josh thought the left wheel must be in a hole or something. All over the plane were rips and tears in the fabric. Sticks and tree branches were poking out everywhere.

Josh was encased in a small opening in the jungle. The trip to make it to the runway would have been as difficult as getting out of the plane. The trees were only a few feet from the tail of the plane, but there seemed to be a wall of brush piled around the back of the plane.

"Well, here it goes," said Josh.

He pressed up against the side of the plane and slid toward the opening. The harder he pressed against the trees and vines, the harder the brush pushed him back. When he got to the vertical stabilizer, he had only ten more feet to the clearing. He started from the back of the plane and got into a big clump of sawgrass.

Josh pulled the collar of his shirt up and tilted his hat forward to protect his face, then forced his way through. The grass cut his hands and arms. It even made a few slits in his shirt. The harder he pushed, the more cuts he got. When he passed the sawgrass there was a jumble of vines. He pressed so firmly on the sawgrass that when it released him, he tumbled into the snarl of vines and sticks. He rolled over on his back and looked up at the sky.

Josh lay there thinking about what his mom would say when the Anderson's called her again and said he didn't show up. What would she do? Would his dad come and rescue him? He didn't know where he was, so how would his dad?

"I can't think about that stuff right now." Josh pushed himself up off the ground.

This time he slowly made his way through the twisted vines. When he pressed through the final two feet, he caught his shirt on a twig and ripped the side of it open up to his armpit. Josh stood up straight and looked down the runway. The small jungle growth was bent and twisted in every direction.

He turned around and looked at his airplane. The left wing went clear down and rested on the ground. The wing tip disappeared into the tangle of the jungle. The right wing stuck up in the air and the whole plane was covered with slits and tears from the sticks and parts of the trees.

He was hoping he could pull the airplane out of the brush, patch some holes, and get it airborne again, but there were far too many holes to patch and the plane leaned too far to the left. He hoped the wheel was in a hole or something.

Josh shook his head. He loved that airplane and here it sat in the middle of nowhere, wrecked. He decided to walk down the runway to see what had caused the airplane to turn off into the trees.

The bushes and small trees were bent over facing the opposite direction. Some of them were broken off, but most of them were just bent over.

Josh walked down the right side, looking for what had caused the accident. The runway looked like it had the center chopped down. About halfway down there were two tire marks and then a mowed down, jumbled area that went into the trees. That transition is where he would check to see what he had hit.

He walked down about two hundred feet. Sticking out of the brush was a white piece of aircraft tubing. As Josh walked up to it he saw it was not just a piece of tubing, it was the entire landing gear strut from the left side of his plane. Attached to the end of the strut was the wheel and tire. He looked around to see what it had hit. There it was about ten feet back! A large boulder had been hidden by the bushes and small trees. The rock was so big it didn't move when it was hit. The scrape marks on the top let Josh know this was the culprit.

The broken strut made Josh realize his dreams of patching the plane and getting it out of there were over. He would need a few men and a truck or a helicopter to get it out. Josh had to change his thinking of how he was going to get out of here. He knew his dad would come looking for him. He also knew he would have to spend the night in the jungle alone—again.

His father had taught him to stay with the airplane if something happened. But where was he? He knew what route he was flying before the engine quit, but then he had turned off to land on this abandoned road. He had never been here before. He had not seen a village, town, or road. There had been no sign of any people for at least a half hour. All he knew was that he was in the middle of the jungle and there was no one around. That thought scared him.

"Father, give me courage to face what I have to. Thank You that I was not injured in the wreck. Help my dad to find me tomorrow. Father, protect the Anderson's kid and give them the peace and comfort they need. Please heal his sickness, give me wisdom to know what I need, and show me what You want me to do."

When Josh opened his eyes he was struck by the beauty of the jungle. God created a beautiful thing! Josh laughed at himself. He was beginning to be just like his dad, always thankful for the beauty of creation.

As Josh walked back down to his airplane, he kept listening to the sky for another plane. He realized it was too early for anyone to be out looking for him, but he couldn't help himself. He wondered what he could do to get someone to notice him from the air, if there was anyone flying anywhere. He had nothing to mark his crash site. No blanket, no banner—nothing. All he had was the fabric on the airplane. He didn't want to damage the plane any more than it already was.

The plane looked worse when he got back. Every square inch was poked or torn. He decided he would try to take the fabric off the top of the wings. He hoped he could get it off in big enough pieces to make a sign.

Josh reached in his pocket and pulled out his Swiss Army knife. The way back into the airplane was easier this time. He had pushed enough of the brush out of the way. When Josh got to the side of the fuselage, he thought the "N" number on the side might help his dad recognize it as his crash site.

"Well, here it goes. Sorry about this," Josh said like he was talking to a person. What an odd thing to do. He wouldn't do that anymore.

Josh poked the blade of his knife into the side of the airplane and pulled it along a horizontal line until it hit one of the cross braces inside. He pulled his knife out, moved it to the other side of the tubing, and stuck it in again. He repeated that all the way down the side of the plane. Then he moved the knife down to the bottom and did it all the way down the side of the plane again.

With that done he cut two vertical lines: one on each end of the sign. The fabric was now loose, so Josh went to all the cross braces, pulled out the fabric, and cut it. When that was done the fabric with the number fell to the ground. He rolled it up and took it out to the runway.

After clearing all the brush away, he unrolled the material and placed it on the ground with the "N" number showing. Then he found four small rocks and placed one on each corner of the fabric. He went back to the airplane and started to cut the fabric off the bottom side of the wings. Then he carefully cut the fabric into strips about two feet long. Josh gathered up all the strips and headed back out to the clearing near the "N" number sign.

Josh took the strips and started to spell the word, "HELP." He had enough material to write "HEL" and half of the "P." He went back to the plane to cut the rest of the letter. With that done, he went back out and finished the letter. Now anyone could see there was someone who needed to be rescued.

When Josh looked up, he realized it was starting to get dark. He decided to light a fire next to his sign so someone could see it at night and it would make him feel more secure in the dark. The last time he spent the night alone in the jungle it was raining. At least this time it was clear.

Josh spent the remaining minutes of light gathering all the firewood he would need for the night. He lit the fire and when it burned on its own, he sat down next to it and waited.

Josh knew his mother would be worried when he didn't come home that night. He wished he could get a message to her, but he couldn't. He couldn't get a message to anyone. All he could do was wait and pray.

"Father, my mother is going to cry all night. Please reassure her that everything is all right. Well, almost everything. Give her peace and comfort her. Bring my dad home so he can find me tomorrow. Teach me what You want me to learn in this. In Jesus' name, amen."

Josh sat and stared into the fire for a long time.

"I sure hope my dad comes tomorrow."

CHAPTER 2

When it started to get dark, Liz Powers started to worry. Joshua had never been gone all night without telling them. He had always called or something. When it finally got dark, she fell to her knees and started to pray and cry. She was on her knees in front of the couch until Josh's dad got home the next morning.

Doug Powers had flown in from Honduras that morning expecting to see his family. When he found Liz on her knees, it worried him.

"Where's Joshua's airplane? Is Joshua here?" Doug asked.

"Joshua didn't come home last night," Liz sobbed. "He flew over to the Anderson's in Guatemala and didn't come home."

"What was he doing at the Anderson's?"

"Their son is real sick and needed a plane to take him to a hospital. You were gone and Joshua was bored, so I sent him. He wanted to be just like his dad and fly for people in need."

"Have you tried calling the Anderson's on the radio?"

"I tried last night, but didn't get anyone." Liz had tears streaming down her face.

"I'll go try again. Maybe I'll radio the MacFee's and have them contact the Anderson's to see what we can learn." Doug walked toward the radio room.

Doug came back in twenty minutes. The look on his face wasn't good and Liz started to cry again.

"The Anderson's said he never showed up or heard a word from him. I'm going to look for him. He's all right. I know the approximate route he had to fly to get over there, so I'll fly the same one. I'll find him."

Doug walked over to where Liz was kneeling in front of the couch and got down on his knees beside her. He put his arms around her and closed his eyes.

"Heavenly Father, You know what it is like to lose a son. You know that our hearts are heavy and we want to know where he is. Father, give us wisdom today to look and place Your hope in our hearts. I know You have a plan in all this, no matter the outcome. Help us to see Your plan and not ours. Comfort our hearts as we search. In Your Son's precious name, amen."

Tears were rolling down Doug's cheeks when Liz looked at him.

"Doug, I am sure Joshua is ok."

"I hope so. I'm going out now to look for him. Try to get some sleep," Doug choked out as he got up. He pulled Liz up to him and they hugged.

"No, I am going with you. You need someone to look out the right side of the plane. If I get tired, I'll take a nap in the plane."

Doug nodded and walked out to fuel the plane. Liz gathered up a few granola bars for breakfast and filled two plastic bottles with water.

When Liz walked out to the plane, Doug was up on the ladder screwing the cap back on the fuel tank. He crawled off the ladder, took it over by the pump, and laid it on the ground, then went and unhooked the ground wire from the plane. When he walked back to the airplane he reached down and removed the chock from the wheel.

"Are you ready?"

Liz climbed onto the co-pilot's seat of the Cessna Caravan and shut the door. Doug crawled onto the pilot's seat and picked up his checklist. In his frame of mind, he didn't want to forget anything. All he wanted was to find his son.

The whine and roar of the turbine engine started to settle him down. Doug taxied the plane out to the end and turned around on the runway. Without any hesitation, he pushed the throttle forward and started his takeoff roll. The airplane rolled down the runway, gaining speed on the hard packed dirt surface. When it lifted into the air, Doug started a slow turn to two hundred sixty degrees.

"This is, probably, the heading Joshua flew over to the Anderson's." Doug looked over at his wife. There were tears rolling down her cheeks as she sat and cried silently.

"We'll find him," Doug said softly into his microphone. "We will find him."

They flew the hour over to the Indian village where the Anderson's were living. The whole village consisted of ten palm frond huts and a dirt airstrip in the middle of the jungle. There was nothing around the village for fifty miles.

"I think we better land and ask the Anderson's if they can tell us anything, and check on their son," said Liz.

Doug pulled back on the throttle and put the flaps down. The plane slowed and started the descent. When he was lined up with the runway, he put the flaps all the way down. The airplane slid down to the ground in the still morning air. They taxied up the remaining part of the runway and parked out in front of the Anderson's hut. Liz opened the co-pilot's door and flipped the ladder down before the engine had stopped turning.

Jill Anderson came out of the hut with her baby on her hip. She walked up to Liz and put her free arm around her.

"I am so sorry. Have you received any new information about Joshua?" said Jill.

Liz couldn't speak and just shook her head. She finally choked out, "How is your son doing?"

"His fever broke yesterday about noon. He got up this morning and is off with his dad," Jill said. "He's acting like nothing happened."

"Praise God!" said Doug. "Can you tell us anything, anything at all, about Joshua? Did you see or even hear anything yesterday?"

"I am so sorry, I didn't," said Jill as she hugged Liz again.

"I didn't think so. Just thought we should stop in and ask, and find out about your son," said Doug. "We'll keep looking. We are going to find Joshua."

"Let me pray with you," said Jill. "Dear heavenly Father, comfort Liz and Doug as they go about their search for their lost son. I know how hard that…" Jill stopped and choked back her tears. "Father, give them peace as they look. Guard Joshua while he is out in the jungle somewhere. Lead them to him. We thank You for Your love for us. In Jesus' name, amen." Jill hugged Liz again then turned and hugged Doug.

"We will find him," said Doug.

"I hope so."

They got back into the airplane and started the engine. Doug turned the plane around and taxied to the end of the runway. Swinging the plane around, Doug pushed the throttle forward, and the plane started down the strip. When they got almost to the end of the runway, the plane lifted into the air.

"Look for any road or place where you might think an airplane could land," said Doug.

Liz nodded and looked out the side window.

They flew back, checking every road or trail they could see. Doug glanced to the ground to see a tree or house or something he could reference for the return trip. Every place they went led to nothing.

"Fuels getting low," said Liz.

Doug checked his fuel gauge and saw it was indeed getting low. He silently nodded his head.

"I think we better head straight home and get more fuel. I'll fly back out and search until dark."

Liz nodded, afraid to speak because she might start crying again. Doug cut back on the power to save fuel.

"Let's keep looking and point out anyplace you see. When I come back, I'll get a closer look."

They flew on for fifteen minutes without saying a word. There was nothing on the ground expect trees. They didn't see trails, roads, or any place that even looked like a plane had landed or could land if necessary.

Liz was looking at all the trees and then she spotted it. In the distance, she saw a faint stripe in the jungle.

"There! Over there! There's a place over there," said Liz.

Doug looked out through the late afternoon sun. It was so far away in the bright sunlight that Doug couldn't see it.

"I can't see where you are talking about. Where is it?"

"Look straight out my window. Follow the line of the wing. It is just about at the wing tip."

Doug's eyes followed the wing out to the end. There in the distance, he saw the road or whatever it had been.

"I see it. I'll check that out when I come back. I think it is too far off course, but I will check it out."

Josh heard the airplane off in the distance. He came out from under the trees and searched the sky. When he finally found it, the plane looked to be five or six miles away.

He could tell it was the Caravan.

"Dad? Dad, over here!" Josh yelled as he jumped up and down, waving his arms. He turned and looked at his fire, but it had gone out. It was not even smoking.

The plane just continued on its path. Josh knew his dad couldn't see him because of all the trees, but he hoped he would come back and look again. At least he knew his dad was looking. It would just be a matter of time. His dad had other pilots in the area he could call on to help look. Someone would find him.

The beautiful day turned into a rainy day. The water started down so hard that Josh had to run back to the plane and crawl inside. The gas was still trickling down the tree from the ruptured tank. That made him nervous, but at least it was getting diluted from all the rain.

Josh started to think about his life. He knew he wanted to fly, but did he want to be a missionary pilot or maybe work his way up to fly for an airline? God had been good to him all of his life. Every time he had a problem with an airplane or people, God had protected him. His life had always been filled with love and compassion from his parents. From his life as a missionary kid, he also knew there was a lot more to life than money.

Josh had always been intrigued by the Bible story of Peter when Jesus called him. Peter had a successful fishing business. One day he was out mending his nets, when Jesus walked up to him and said, "Peter, follow Me." Did Peter know Jesus before this? Peter didn't say, "Jesus, I have a successful business here. It's the livelihood for my family. You know I have a wife and her mother, maybe even kids I need to take care of. Come back in ten years and it will be different then." He didn't say anything like this. All he did was do what Jesus asked of him. He got up right then, left his boat, left the net, and the people who worked for him, and followed Jesus.

He failed sometimes, but he followed Him to death. That's what Doug Powers was trying to do. Follow Jesus the best he could. Josh wanted to be like his dad, but he didn't want to be a missionary pilot just because his dad was one. He wanted to follow Jesus in whatever He asked him to do. Even if that meant not flying and doing something else.

Father, You know the situation I'm in. I want to do whatever You have for me in life. I want to follow You like Peter did and be a witness and testimony of Your love for the world. Whatever You want me to do, even if it is not flying, I will do it. Help me figure out what I should do to be rescued. Give me Your peace and comfort while I wait. In Jesus' name, amen.

All Josh could hear was the roar of the rain on the jungle canopy and the rain hitting the wreckage of the airplane. He was glad the cockpit was watertight. At least he was out of the rain.

It was starting to get dark outside and the rain didn't stop. Josh decided to sleep in the airplane, but he didn't know how much sleep he would get. He crawled onto the back seat and stretched out as much as he could. He turned from side to side, trying to get comfortable, but it didn't work. He lay cramped on the back seat for what seemed like hours, listening to the rain.

Suddenly, the whole inside of the airplane was illuminated with a bright, white flash, followed by a crack that ended in a roar of loud thunder. The lightshow and thunder went on for hours. Just when Josh would fall asleep, the light would flash so brightly that he would open his eyes and be blasted by the noise. He wouldn't get much sleep that night.

CHAPTER 3

The sound of an airplane going overhead a few hundred feet woke Josh from his sound sleep. It had to be his dad looking for him. He tried to get out of the cockpit as quickly as he could, but the door still didn't open right. He started his legs under the top door and tried to push himself through. His shirt somehow got tangled with the control stick in the back seat. He had to pull himself back into the airplane and try to get untangled.

Josh had to sit back up in the seat to get free. This time he decided to go out sitting upright. He pushed his feet out under the door again and eased his way toward the exit, making sure his shirt didn't get snagged again. When his legs were finally free, he had to bend his back backwards to get to the ground.

When he finally touched the ground, he tried to hurry so he wouldn't miss his dad. The land was a soggy, slick mess and his feet wouldn't hold. His muddy boots slipped out from under him and he scraped all the way down his back as he slammed his head on the edge of the bottom door. He tumbled to the muddy ground and landed flat on his back, banging his head on a small rock.

Josh was stunned. He tried to get up, but fell back down. He lay there on the cold, wet, muddy ground for what seemed like an eternity. He reached up, grabbed the bottom of the door, and pulled himself up to a sitting position. When his head cleared, Josh pulled himself up on the wreckage of the airplane.

Josh stumbled from tree to tree, trying to get out to the landing strip where his dad could see him. His dad had to have seen the "N" number and the word "HELP" he had stretched out on the ground the day before. It was only a matter of time now.

Josh could hear the airplane coming around again. He struggled through the trees, trying to get out where his dad could see him. He wanted him to know he was still alive and the only way he could do that was for his dad to see him.

When Josh got to the edge of the trees, he saw the tail of his dad's airplane flying across the landing strip.

"Dad! Dad, down here!" Josh jumped up and down, waving both his arms above his head. He knew his dad couldn't hear or see him, but he had to try.

The plane was right above him and going over a hundred and twenty miles per hour. He knew his dad couldn't see him from that position, but he was sure his dad knew where he was. The signs had to tell him. That's why his dad came back again.

Josh moved out onto the middle of the landing strip and stood there waiting for his dad to come back. The sun was beating down on his aching head and the dirty, torn shirt on his back was starting to dry. He shielded his eyes from the morning sun, looked, and waited.

Josh was thirsty and didn't have any water to drink. Every place he looked there were puddles of water. Brown, filthy water. He decided to wait for his dad and a short trip home where he could drink all the clean, fresh water he wanted.

The minutes turned into hours as Josh waited. Maybe his dad saw where he was and went home to get something— a Jeep, or an airplane, or something to come out and get him. Josh decided to sit down under the trees in the shade and wait.

As he sat there under the trees, trying to keep the ants off, he wondered where he was. He thought he had left Belize and was in Guatemala, but he wasn't sure. There didn't seem to be any roads around or anything. The place he had landed was a strip cut out of the jungle for something, but there was no way to get to it other than by air. Maybe it was an airport someone was going to make and ran into trouble.

That was an exciting idea for Josh. Trouble. There was a landing strip in the middle of nowhere that someone had abandoned because of some problem, but it saved his life. But now he was having trouble. Did the children of Israel feel they were in trouble when they were in the wilderness? They didn't want to die out there after God showed them the Promised Land. He would have to keep that in mind while he waited to be rescued.

Josh couldn't wait for his dad to get back and pick him up. As close as his dad was the last time he flew over, he had to have seen the markers. The "N" and the "HELP" sign were big and enough contrast to the green jungle that he had to have seen them.

Josh didn't want to sit there all day, but he thought he better hang around the airplane until his dad came back. He stood up, stretched, and walked out from under trees.

The sun was blazing hot and felt like it was eating his bare arms and head. He had to get something to at least cover his head. He walked back to the wreckage of the airplane and looked for his hat or something to cover his head. He couldn't find his hat anywhere.

While he rummaged around in the plane, he found an old towel he had used to wipe the dipstick when he checked his oil. It had two dirty, black, oily stripes running down one side and a small hole in the other end.

"This will do." Josh placed the towel over his head and began to look for something to tie it on. He looked behind the back seat and found a small bundle of army-green parachute cord. He pulled out his knife and cut three pieces about two and a half feet long. Then he tied the ends of the sections together and hooked that on the door handle of the plane. Very carefully he braided the three pieces together. Then he tied the other end.

With that done, he cornered the towel, wrapped the braided parachute cord around his head, and tied it in the back. The sides of the towel covered the sides and back of his neck, but it didn't do much for his face. It would have to do for now.

Josh's mouth was starting to get dry. He had not had a drink of water for hours. He went back to the plane and looked for the bottle of water he had when the plane went down. He looked for the plastic cup holder on the left side of the cockpit. The container of water and the cup holder were both gone.

Josh looked everywhere. He checked under the seat and around the floor in the back. Nothing! He was puzzled by the disappearance. When he started to slide out of the plane, a glint of silver caught his eye. Down beneath the dashboard, stuck behind the left rudder peddle was the bottle of water still in the cup holder. When he got it out, he was surprised at how much water was missing. There was about one inch of water in the sixteen ounce bottle. That would have to do for now. He figured his dad would be there before he needed another drink.

He waited for hours for his dad to return. He went and sat under a tree, but then he would get tired of that and would get up and pace. He went back and crawled into the airplane to take a short nap. By then, most of the day was gone and it was starting to get dark.

Josh had to get up and gather some wood for a fire. When he walked out into the jungle, the first of the daily rainstorms started. At first, it was only a few large drops, but the rain increased from there. After five minutes of wood gathering, it was raining so hard he couldn't see twenty-five yards. He was soaked to the skin.

As hot and steamy as it was during the day, Josh knew it would be a cold night. He was soaked with nowhere to go except back into the leaky wreckage of the airplane. If the rain didn't stop in five minutes, there would be no fire tonight, and he would have a hard time staying warm until morning.

As Josh walked back toward his downed airplane, he realized the rain would be a good time to fill his water bottle. He looked for a smooth, green leaf on a plant. He could cut the whole leaf off so he wouldn't have to deal with the goo inside. When he found the right leaf, he pulled out his pocket knife and cut the stem of the leaf. He held up the leaf to the rain and got it wet enough so he could wash off all the dirt. Then he rolled it up to make a funnel and stuck it in the top of his water bottle.

With that done, he walked out onto the runway and put the bottle on the ground with the funnel facing up. The weight of the funnel tipped the bottle over and the leaf got muddy.

Josh gathered up a couple of rocks and put them on both sides of the bottle to make it stable. He took the leaf, washed the mud off in the rain, and placed it back in the bottle. He stood and watched the bottle for a couple of minutes, and then went back to the airplane and crawled inside.

Josh bowed his head. "Dear Father, You know the situation I'm in. You know that all I can do is wait for my dad to come and get me. Please give me the patience to wait. Lord, thank You for protection thus far. In Jesus' name, amen."

The minutes seemed like hours as Josh waited. The roar of the rain was relentless. Sometimes the noise would be so loud that he couldn't think. The drips inside the plane started getting worse. He had to sit in a strange position to keep himself from getting wetter. His back was beginning to hurt from sitting all twisted up.

A crash of thunder made Josh jump and he bumped his head against the side window. The lightning was so close and the thunder so loud that he thought it had struck the airplane. The flashes happened every thirty seconds for the next hour. They would bring passing daylight to the blackness of the night. All Josh could do was sit there and try to wait out the storm. There wouldn't be any sleep that night until the lightning storm was over.

When morning finally came, Josh couldn't believe he got any sleep at all. He didn't remember the lightning stopping or anything else. The grayness of the dawn let him know his wait had started all over again. He decided he would explore around the airport as he waited for his dad.

He slipped out of the cockpit onto the soggy, muddy ground. He held onto the plane so he wouldn't repeat what happened last time. The mud clung to the bottom of his boots as he slipped away from the aircraft.

The first thing he did when he got out from under the trees was to walk directly to the bottle he had put out in the open when it had started to rain. The bottle was sitting in the middle of a giant puddle of muddy brown water. The dirty water was clear up to the neck, but none had gotten in. He waded carefully out into the water so he wouldn't make any waves and splash dirty water inside the bottle.

Josh picked up the bottle and pulled the leaf funnel out. His thirst was overwhelming as he put the bottle up to his lips and took a large gulp. The bitter taste of the water made him spit it out. The leaf he'd chosen for the funnel had left a bad taste. It was so strong he couldn't take it even if he wanted to. He sipped it again and it made him gag. Josh reluctantly poured the rest of it into the puddle. He hoped it was not poisonous. He would have to wait and see. He would be more careful next time.

He looked at both ends of the runway. He knew what was down to his right, or at least he thought he did. He decided to go down to the left end of the strip to see if he could see anybody or anything. If there was an Indian village, maybe he could get a message out to the world.

Josh started down toward the end of the runway. The sun was intense on his head. The towel didn't help much. It felt like it was cooking his brain inside his head. The lack of water was starting to get to him. He hoped he could find a clear stream to get a fresh drink of water. He knew he would be taking a chance drinking out of any stream, but he was getting too thirsty.

The end of the runway was covered with jungle trees and brush. The tangle of brush made him stop and think. If his dad came for him, he would hear the truck or airplane long before it got there and he could come out of the trees. His dad would see him on the runway and it would be over, but until then he would have to look for water.

Josh pushed his way into the brush. The tangle let go into a tree covered area where the ground was clear. He checked his watch and the sun so he would know which direction he was going. He would keep heading south, directly off the end of the airstrip. Josh did the best he could to mark the trail with bent grass and broken branches so he could find his way back.

He walked for a quarter of a mile and when he broke out of the brush he came to the edge of a giant river. The river was big and full, and running fast. The rain the night before had brought the river up. He would not be able to cross this river for a few days, but he hoped his dad would be there to pick him up before then.

Josh's mouth was dry and his body wanted water. He looked at the river. The pool was muddy and brown, but he thought he could strain the dirt out. He pulled the empty bottle out of his pocket and looked for a good spot on the water's edge. There were little inlets with water standing almost still. He got down and plunged the bottle into the water. When it was half full, he noticed a dead bug floating at the edge.

Josh stood up and poured the water back into the river. He knew he might get a little sick from drinking this water, but the dead bug was going too far. He looked around for another place he could fill his bottle. When he found the inlet where the water was still, he bent over and cleared out all of the debris. When the water settled down, he stuck the lip of the bottle half underwater. The bottle filled slowly with brown water.

He set the bottle down on a rock and let the dirt settle to the bottom of the bottle. While he waited, he thought about giardia or cholera. He had heard people talk about these diseases, but he didn't know anything about either one. He just knew you could get sick from drinking dirty, tainted water.

Josh watched the bottle as long as his thirst would let him. He gently picked it up and tried not to stir it. Very carefully he raised the water to his lips and tipped it slowly. He worked hard not to get any of the sediment in his mouth.

The cold river water felt so good going down his throat! He stopped when it got to the sediment and poured the dirt out. He stuck the bottle back into the water and let it fill again. This time he didn't wait for it to settle. He looked at the color of the water and thought it was almost clean.

"Well, here it goes," Josh said as he drank the whole bottle of water. He felt it quench his thirst. He couldn't resist. He filled the bottle again and sucked the water out of it.

"That's so good! I hope I don't get sick." The water ran down his chin and dripped onto the front of his shirt. His hand went up and wiped off the flecks of mud.

Josh walked over to a tree and stood in the shade. He looked out at the river and thought about how beautiful it was. The water was running smooth and full. It was so deep that the rocks were underwater. The river was moving at a breakneck pace. Josh scanned the riverbank and then he saw them.

Across the river were Indian children playing in the shallow water. Josh ran out to the edge of the water and started to wave both hands.

"Here, over here!" The children froze. Two little girls disappeared into the jungle. The boys retreated to a large bush and peered over the forest at Josh. Three of the boys slipped off into the darkness. Only one of them held his place, keeping watch.

"Wait! I crashed a plane over here and do not know where I am." Josh could see the boy's head sticking up over the bush. "Can you tell me where I am?" The boy finally started to move off into the jungle.

"Wait! Don't go! Wait!" was all Josh could get out of his mouth before the boy was gone. He stood staring at the spot where he had seen them. He wondered if they would tell their parents that they saw a stranger down by the river. He decided to sit and wait for a few minutes.

After ten minutes of waiting an old man dressed only in shorts came out of the jungle. Josh jumped to his feet and came out from under the tree.

"Hey! Over here!" Josh jumped up and down, waving his arms. The man turned and waved at Josh. He started talking, but Josh couldn't understand him. The man was speaking Kekchi.

"Do you speak English?" The man kept talking and waving his arms.

Josh understood from the man waving his arms and other gestures that there was no way for him to get across the river at flood stage. The man kept pointing off toward the runway. He must have figured there was someone over in that direction that could help.

The man stopped talking and after a pause said one last thing, waved, and then disappeared into the jungle.

CHAPTER 4

Josh stood there looking at the spot where the man had been. There was no way for him to get across the river. The water was moving much too fast to swim and he didn't see a boat that he could use. Crossing the river was out.

He filled his water bottle, turned, and started back through the jungle. He looked for the tree branches and grass he had broken to find his way. That made getting back to the runway easy. When he broke out onto the airstrip, he couldn't see his airplane. He wondered if his dad could see it from the air.

Josh walked back to the airplane and sat down under a tree. As soon as he sat down, the ants started to bite. He jumped up and brushed himself off. He decided he would walk down to the other end of the runway and see what was down there. He would stay out in the clearing so if his dad came back he would be able to see him.

He walked out to the strip and started down toward the end. He marched one hundred yards and then realized he didn't see his signs. Josh went back where he thought he had put them. They weren't there. He started to walk in a circle around the place he thought they were. He couldn't find them anywhere. When he finally located the exact spot, there was a giant, thick, dark brown puddle of water. It was so dark he couldn't see the bottom. He waded out into the water and tried to locate the "HELP" sign.

Josh put his hand down into the muddy water and felt around for the material. All he could find was one strip. The rest of it was gone. He ran over to the place he thought he had put the "N" number. The wind had crumpled it up and blown it under some of the bushes. Josh couldn't believe this had happened. Both signs were now covered up.

"Oh, man! I sure hope my dad saw them before this happened." Josh stood there, staring at the crumpled up signs. If his dad hadn't seen them, then Josh was out here all alone with no one coming to get him. His dad had taught him to stay with the airplane and someone would come. They would come if they knew where the aircraft was located. But his plane was off the runway, back in the trees. His dad had his back to the crashed plane when he went over. The direction he was going he would not have seen the airplane.

"Heavenly Father, You know this is a huge disappointment to me. What am I to do? I need Your perfect plan. Should I keep waiting for my dad or should I go try to find my way out? Amen."

Josh decided he would spend that night out in the forest. If his dad didn't come, he would try to figure out what to do. He stood there staring at the crumpled sign. He couldn't believe the wind and rain had wiped out his plans for rescue. He bent over and picked up the cloth with the "N" number, then spread it out on the ground. He looked for big rocks to hold down the corners. He searched for foundations for a half hour and didn't find any.

He went back to the airplane and spotted some tree branches that had broken off when the aircraft plowed through the trees. Josh picked up two of them and started back toward the sign. Both of the branches were heavy and one of them began to twist. It turned around his body and smacked him in the chin.

Josh dropped both branches and rubbed his chin. When he brought his hand down, he had a smear of blood. He wiped his chin again, picked up one of the branches, and started for the sign. When he got out by the material, he dropped the branch on one end and wiped his chin again.

Josh caught movement out of the corner of his eye just as he heard the distinct sound of a turbine engine on an airplane. There hadn't been Maya or Tropic Airlines flying over, so he knew it had to be his dad. The plane was flying the same route he was on when his engine had quit. It was a long way off, but Josh had to try something. He started to jump up and down and scream. He waved both arms to make enough movement. Any movement at all should catch his dad's attention, and Josh hoped he would see him.

He reached down and tried to grab the "N" number sign so he could wave it. The branch he had just laid down snagged on one end and he couldn't get it up. When he looked back up for the airplane, it was gone. Josh's shoulders slumped down and he dropped the sign. He stood there staring at where the plane had been.

Josh knew his dad would have to fly back. It should take him forty minutes to get to the Anderson's and forty minutes back. He would be waiting. He straightened the sign out on the ground and put the branch back on. Then he went to the other branch, carried it over to the sign, and placed it on the other end.

Josh went and sat on a fallen log in the shade. His mind kept going to the children of Israel and their struggle in the wilderness. How hard that would have been since no one was coming to rescue them. And they were in the middle of the desert with no shade. He thought that would be the worst thing he could think of. But at least they weren't alone.

The whistling sound of a turbine engine caught his attention. Josh jumped off the log and ran out to the runway just in time to see his father's airplane disappear behind the trees. His dad was right down on the tops of the trees, clear down at the end of the runway.

Josh jerked the towel off his head and started to wave. "Dad! Dad, I'm here!" That was all he got out before the airplane disappeared. He wondered if his dad caught sight of the movement before it had been too late. He stood in one place with the towel at ready, waiting to see.

After an hour in the sun, he started to get a headache. Josh slowly put the towel back on his head and looked around on the ground for the braided cord. He found it hanging on a bush and blowing in the breeze. Josh picked it up and pulled it onto his head. His face was sunburned and he was thirsty. He felt like his lips were cracked and sun-baked.

Josh looked around for his plastic water bottle with the water from the river. He went back in the shade to the airplane and looked on the seat. The bottle was laying on its side on the pilot's seat. Half of the water had dripped out through a tiny hole up by the neck. He grabbed the bottle and fumbled with the cap. When it was open, he gulped the remaining water. It felt better than it tasted. He would have to save the bottle for more water later, so he tossed it back onto the seat.

The day was the hottest Josh had ever felt. Giant storm clouds were coming his way and the humidity was terrible. He knew he had to gather wood for a fire that night, but if it rained like it did the night before, it would put the fire out. He had to rest out of the sun for a while, so he sat down under a tree and leaned up against it.

The stinging on his neck woke Josh up. He slapped at the insect that had stung him and jumped to his feet. He was covered with ants. He went into a dance, trying to get them off him. He brushed them all off his body. The one bite on his neck was enough for him.

Josh realized he had been asleep for a couple of hours. The storm clouds were now overhead, but there was no rain—not yet anyway. He walked back into the jungle, looking for small pieces of wood that he could carry out to the middle of the runway. He gathered enough wood to make a fire that would last all night.

I wonder where the children of Israel got their firewood out in the wilderness? They were in the middle of the desert with only a few small bushes and they had lots of people. Didn't God have them out there to punish them?

His mind kept working on questions like these. He didn't know why, but he figured he was being punished for something he had done, like the children of Israel.

If the children of Israel could make it forty years, then I can last a few more days.

The next thing he had to do was get the matches he used the first time and light a fire. Someone would see the smoke. Josh felt in his pockets for the matches. They weren't there. He hiked back to the plane and looked for the matches. He looked in the survival kit and didn't find any. He wondered what had happened to them. Josh walked back out to his fire pit and searched all around. There on one of the rocks was the remains of the burnt matchbox.

"Sorry, Dad. I broke the rule. 'Don't lay things down where you can't find them.'" Back at the airplane, Josh slid onto the seat and sat there trying to think what he should do. If he had flint and steel, he could use that, but he didn't have either one. He could make a bow out of a stick and one of the laces in his boots, and try to light a fire that way.

Josh unlaced one of his boots and pulled the string out. Then he looked for a stick about two feet long. He tied one end of the lace to the stick, bent it, then tied the free end of the lace to the opposite side of the stick. He had his bow.

Josh picked up a piece of hardwood about six inches long and took out his pocket knife. He carved one end of the short stick into a point. Then he found a piece of wood that he could use to drill for the fire. With his pocket knife, he carved a depression into the wood and cut a slit in the side of the hole. He looked around and found some dried grass and small sticks to feed the fire once it was going.

After Josh had wrapped the boot lace around the spindle, he realized he needed a block or something to press the spindle down into the wood he was going to light on fire. He looked around and found a piece that was too long. He opened the saw blade on his knife and started to cut the piece to length. It took him a half hour to cut through the wood.

With that finally done, Josh opened the blade on his knife and cut a hole into the side of the stick so it wouldn't slip off the top of the spindle. He piled the grass around the spindle and the lower block, pressing down on it with a top block, and picked up the bow.

"Here it goes!"

Josh started to move the bow back and forth. It ran rough at first, but then it smoothed out. Just when he thought he had it going right, the bottom wood rolled over and scattered the grass everywhere. He couldn't believe that happened. After gathering all the stuff back together, he put one of his feet on the lower stick to hold it in place and picked up the bow and the spindle.

"Here it goes again!"

He moved the bow slowly at first and then gained speed. The spindle turned in its socket, but nothing was happening. There wasn't any smoke coming out of the lower block like he had seen the survivor guys on TV do. A couple of minutes of the bow moving back and forth, and they had their fire. Where was his fire?

Josh decided he would light a fire this way even if it took him all night. A wooden contraption would not defeat him! He started the bow moving back and forth again. Eventually, he got into a steady rhythm.

Every muscle in his back and shoulders was hurting. His leg was just starting to cramp when the spindle broke through the bottom wood and brought the whole thing to a halt. Josh checked his watch. It had been an hour since he started.

"Oh! How long does this take?"

Josh lay down on his back and moved his arms to try and get the pain out of his back. He stretched out his legs. As he lay there thinking, he decided the wood on the bottom was too soft. He would have to find something harder as soon as the aches were gone.

Lord, what's going on here? Did the children of Israel have this much trouble starting a fire when they were in the wilderness? Father, help me get this thing going. Give me the strength to continue. Amen.

Josh jumped to his feet and started to search for a hard piece of wood to light the fire. When he found one, he began to break it to make it shorter, but decided if it was long he could put some rocks on it so it wouldn't move.

He dragged the piece out to the pile of firewood and pulled out his knife. With the tip of the blade, he wore an indentation down in the wood. He carefully cut a notch in the side, then piled grass over the hole. He went to get something to hold the stick.

He didn't think there were any rocks around except the one he had hit with the airplane, and it was too big. But he had to look. He got up and started to walk in a circle around the pile of firewood. The circle kept getting bigger and bigger.

When he got to the edge of the runway, he went off into the jungle. There on the ground was a pile of rocks and dirt, like a tractor had pushed them off the track or road. Josh picked up the biggest rock he could and started to carry it out.

After about ten feet he decided the rock was too big to carry that far, so he dropped it on the ground. He sighed and went back to the pile. He rummaged through the collection, looking for a rock he could carry. After he found three rocks the size he wanted, he piled them up the side.

Josh picked up the first rock, carried it out to the wood, then dropped it on the ground. He went back and got the other two, carrying them one at a time. With that done, he carefully piled the rocks on the wood to hold it in place. He didn't want the piece of wood to roll over or anything else. All he wanted was a fire.

He picked up his bow and the spindle, and stuck it in the hole. He placed his foot on the log and closed his eyes.

"Father, You know I need a fire and this is the only way I have to start one. Please give me the patience to start the fire. Help it to go fast. Amen. Well, here it goes."

Josh sighed and started to run the bow back and forth. The longer it went, the smoother it got. The piece of wood and the receiving lumber were beginning to get black on both ends. He stopped and piled the grass around the hole at the bottom of the stick.

Josh started the movement with the bow again. He kept drilling in the wood for another half hour. He looked up at the sky and noticed that the clouds were getting lower and darker. When he looked back down, he saw it!

There was a tiny whiff of smoke curling up through the grass. That gave him the energy to run the bow back and forth even faster. The faster he went, the more smoke it produced. He stopped the bow and pulled the stick up out of the hole. He didn't see anything glowing. When he touched the end of the stick, it was hot. He had to run the bow longer and harder if he was going to get the fire.

Josh picked up the bow, wrapped the string around the spindle, and stuck the other end in the hole. He started to run the bow again. It didn't take long for him to see smoke.

When he thought he had enough smoke, he dropped the bow, picked up the grass, and started to blow gently. The smoke in the grass drifted out with every breath until he was left holding the bundle of dry grass. Nothing!

Josh picked up the stick and looked at the end of it. There was still no glowing coal on the end. He grabbed the bow, threaded the string around the stick, put it in the hole, and started the bow again. He didn't want it to get cool. Within minutes it began to smoke.

This time he kept the movement of the bow up until he had a lot of smoke. He decided to be safe and keep the bow going until he saw some coal glowing in the hole.

When the smoke got intense, Josh dropped the bow and bent over. Gently, he started to blow air through the grass. The smoke increased so he blew again. When he could open his eyes, through the smoke, he saw it. There was a tiny glowing ember down in the grass. He blew again and again, and finally the grass burst into flames.

"Yes, yes!" That was all Josh could say. He dropped the grass, picked up tiny pieces of wood, and stacked them around the flame. He didn't want to smother the fire, so he had to take his time and let the wood start to burn.

Then he felt it. The first giant drop of rain struck him on the back of his neck.

"No! No, not now!" Josh tried to cover his little fire with his body. The flames were getting too big for that. His shirt started to smoke and burn his skin.

The flash of lightning and clap of thunder were so close and loud that it blinded Josh for a second. The water felt like it was coming down by the bucket full. Within seconds he was drenched to his skin and his once going fire was now only a ringlet of smoke.

Josh fell backward and watched as the smoke totally disappeared. The rain came down so hard that he could barely see the trees. At least it was a warm rain. He reached up, wiped the water out of his hair, and washed his face off.

"Oh Father, what do You want me to learn?" Josh sat there in the rain for a long time, thinking, *I doubt the children of Israel had to deal with much rain out in the desert.*

CHAPTER 5

Josh sat in the rain looking at the spot where he had started the fire. At least he knew he could start another fire if he had to. The rain was coming down so hard that puddles were starting to form everywhere. His clothes were soaked clear down to his skin. He was so discouraged, he just sat there in the rain.

The sky was getting darker and the wind was starting to blow. After a half hour, Josh climbed up on his feet and staggered back toward the airplane. He saw the "N" number sign blow up against the brush and then fall facedown into a brown puddle of water. *Not again!* He stood and watched the sign sink. *I'll fix it tomorrow.*

Josh checked his watch and it was only four o'clock. Way too early for sleep. As he walked back toward the plane, he walked right through all the puddles because he was already soaked. At the edge of the runway there was one more puddle. He waded out into the dark, muddy water, caught his foot on a root, and tripped. Josh fell face first into the water.

"You've got to be kidding!" he yelled as he pulled his mouth up out of the water. He rolled over in a sitting position in the middle of the puddle and slapped the water. The lightning storm started while he was sitting in the pool. A bright flash of light and a tremendous roar of thunder split the air.

"This is just great!" Josh pulled himself back to his feet and shuffled out of the water. He didn't want to do that again. The lightning continued, striking a tree twenty yards from him and setting the tree on fire. It burned for five minutes, but the rain left only the top of the tree smoldering.

All of the excitement of falling into the water and the lightning sent Josh running toward his plane. Through the trees, Josh could see a fire burning the airplane! As he looked above the trees, he could see the black smoke billowing up into the sky. The right wing of the airplane that had been sticking up into the air had been struck by the first bolt of lightning. The fire had burned down the wing and it was getting very close to the right fuel tank.

Josh turned and ran back toward the runway just as the first tank exploded. A half second later, the leaking left tank did the same. The concussion from the explosion knocked Josh to the ground.

As he lay there on the ground, he thought about his father looking for him. He wished his dad was flying right now so he could see the smoke from the burning airplane. The rain was too hard for that. His dad would be heading home if he was out.

His stomach was starting to hurt. His insides rolled and churned and growled. "Oh, not this, too!" was all he could say. Josh got to his feet and looked around for a place to shelter himself until the storm blew over.

He walked to the other side of the runway, away from the burning trees and the airplane, and walked under a tree. It was raining so hard he could barely see the fire at all. Josh looked for a giant leaf to cover himself and when he found one, he sat down and covered his head. The rain should at least keep the ants off him.

Josh sat under the tree with the rain drumming on the leaf. It was so loud he could not think. All he could do was listen. His stomach was starting to get worse. The pain shot through his stomach and went all the way down. *It must be the lack of food and that water I drank.* He got to his feet, walked back into the jungle, and looked for a private spot. He almost laughed at that, since no one was around. Josh went behind a tree and relieved himself. That seemed to help a little, but it started to worry him.

When he was walking back to his tree, he started to get dizzy. He tripped on a branch, but he caught himself. He stumbled onto the tree, sat down, and covered his head. The dizziness continued and he felt like he was going to pass out. He drifted off to sleep, but woke up an hour later and threw up the brown water he had ingested. When he sat back up, another pain shot through his gut. He felt like he was burning up. Josh knew he would have to go back to that private spot again.

Josh got up the best he could, but his world was spinning around. He staggered back to the tree. When he was through, he started again. Halfway there he began to stumble sideways out of control and fell. The last thing he felt was the cold, muddy water on his chest.

When he woke up, he didn't know where he was. It was dark and he could hear the rain coming down hard, but it was not hitting him. His hand went down and touched the small aluminum square that surrounded the cot he was lying on. He realized his head was propped up on a pillow.

"Dad? Dad, where are you?" Josh could hear someone rustling somewhere above his head. "Dad, is that you? Where are we?"

Josh heard the sound of a man walking to him. He put his face down close to Josh's. The flashlight on his helmet shined right in Josh's eyes so he couldn't see his face. "We have to keep our voices down," the man said in a shallow voice. "They'll hear us."

"Who will hear us?" Josh whispered.

"Guatemalans!" He heard the man shuffle back above his head somewhere.

Josh sat up and his head started to spin. "Oh, I don't feel good." He tried to keep sitting upright, but he was starting to feel the nausea coming back. He laid back down on the cot. "Think I'll stay here a while."

"Get some more sleep if you want, I need to guard the airstrip," the man said. "I'll be right here."

"Why do you have to watch the airstrip?"

The man started to mumble. Josh could only catch a few things he said. There was something about national security…team…Guatemalans, but the rest he couldn't understand. *Is this man all right?*

Josh lay back down and closed his eyes. He thought he should stay awake, but he couldn't. *Father, protect me while I sleep. Thank You for the man who rescued me. Help me to be kind to him and show Your love.*

When Josh opened his eyes, the sun was brightly shining outside. He lay on his bed and took in his surroundings. He was in a palm frond hut like the Kekchi Indians made. The cot he had been sleeping on was the only furniture in the room. There were some old MRE cases and cans thrown into the corner of the hut. Two small rectangular holes were cut through the palm fronds on each wall. The holes were about three feet off the ground. He didn't have the slightest idea what they were for.

He grabbed the edge of the cot, pulled himself up slowly, and turned to look at the man.

The man was sound asleep on his knees by one of the holes and his head was resting on the post next to it. He snored a little. Josh was surprised at how old he was. He looked to be around sixty or seventy years old. He had on a light tan uniform that was tattered and torn. His boots looked like they had seen a thousand miles and their soles were worn down—one of them even had a hole through the bottom. He had on an old flak jacket and his helmet was laying on the floor next to him.

The thing that scared Josh was the guy had an old Vietnam War-era M16 rifle. As he sat there looking the gun over, he noticed that it didn't have a magazine. He looked around everywhere and didn't see any. The guy had a gun but no ammunition.

Josh wondered if he should wake him or leave. Before he could decide, the old man snorted and coughed, then turned and looked at him.

"Feeling better, marine?" The man turned and started to look through the small hole in front of him.

"Yeah, I'm still a little dizzy, but I am doing fine."

"You need something to eat? Get yourself one of the MREs over there and chow down." He never took his eyes off the hole.

Josh got to his feet the best he could. He still felt shaky. He went to the corner of the hut where all of the MREs were thrown in a corner. There must have been fifty army-brown bags. He picked up one sack and read the name of the meal. It said, "omelet with ham." The package contained a tan box with the dried omelet, one that had

[61]

potatoes au gratin, an oatmeal cookie bar, a powdered grape drink, some cheese spread, and a package of crackers that felt like they were bulletproof. None of that sounded very good to him, so he picked up another bag. It was the exact same meal. Every bag he picked up was the same meal.

This will do just fine, he thought. He was so hungry, anything would have sounded good to him, but his stomach was still churning a little. He would try this meal and if it agreed with him, it would be a blessing.

Josh read the instructions and found a little pan and an old Coleman one-burner backpacking stove to heat up the food. When it was ready, he bowed his head. *Father, thank You for this food. Thank You for this man who found me and brought me here to rest. Help my dad find me. Let me do Your will. Amen.*

When he opened his eyes the man was staring at him.

"You praying?" the man asked.

Josh sat there a few seconds before he spoke. "Uh...yes, I was."

The man stared at Josh for about a minute before he spoke. "I used to pray. Back when I was about your age. How old are you, fifteen or sixteen?"

"I'm fifteen, sir," Josh said.

"Don't call me, 'sir.' I'm an enlisted man like you, marine."

"Why don't you pray anymore?" Josh asked.

[62]

The man turned his attention back outside. "The Team is a pretty rough group. They talk bad and do things and have things done to them. You don't always have time. Only when someone gets hurt, then you remember to pray," the man said as he stumbled through his words.

Josh didn't know what to say. He sat there silently eating for a few minutes. "What's your name, mister?"

"I'm Jonathan Michael Banka, but you can call me Scooter. Who might you be?"

"I'm Josh...Joshua Powers. Nice to meet you. How'd you get the name Scooter?"

"That's what the Team called me because I moved so fast when we're moving through the jungle. I'd hurry right along."

"Scooter, how far are we from the airstrip?" Josh asked.

"We're about two hundred yards. I saw the day you landed or crashed out there. Checked on you. When I saw you were ok, I figured someone would come and get you. When lightning struck your plane and you passed out, that's when I came and got you. Where were you going anyway?"

"I was on my way over to the Anderson's in Guatemala to pick up their son to take him to the doctor, but then my engine froze."

"Yours was the only plane to try to land on that strip. Who are the Anderson's?"

[63]

"They're a missionary couple living in a Mayan Indian village," Josh said.

"I know those people. The Team made contact with them a few years back. We're about a quarter of a mile inside Belize and they were about forty miles inside Guatemala. Well, get some sleep and I'll take you to them in the morning."

"Sounds good!" said Josh. By then he had finished his breakfast. While they were talking, he had been praying that God would give him an opening so he could share the Lord with him.

"Did you go to church when you were my age?" Josh asked.

Scooter looked at him, then turned and looked out the hole in the wall of the hut. He sat silent for a long time.

"I used to. But that was a long time and a lot of wars ago."

"Do you believe that Jesus loves you?" Josh asked, looking down at the ground.

Scooter turned, looked down at his boots, and sat there staring at them for a long time. Finally, he said, "I used to, but I don't know how He could now. All of the bad stuff that I have done and the things I did with the Team…"

"The Bible says that all of us have sinned and fallen short of the glory of God," Josh said softly.

"I don't have enough years left to do good to get Jesus to recognize how sorry I am for all I have done and I am doing," said Scooter.

"It is not a matter of being good enough; it is God's grace that saves us. All we have to do is believe. We have to have faith, and that is a gift of God," said Josh.

"Faith, huh? I only have faith in things I can see and touch, like my Seal Team members I fought with," Scooter growled. "I don't want to talk about this right now."

Josh didn't know what to say to that. "But God says…"

"I don't want to talk about it anymore," Scooter said in a way that sounded like a command. "I'm going out on patrol. You rest up. I'll take you to your people tomorrow."

Scooter wouldn't look at Josh. He picked up his harmless weapon and canteen, peeked out the door, and snuck out into the jungle. Josh sat down on the cot and closed his eyes.

Father, help me say the right thing to Scooter. Give me patience to speak Your truth. Give me Your words at the right time. I know You want him saved. Please soften his heart. In Jesus' name…amen.

Josh lay back on the cot and put his feet up. He hadn't realized how tired he was. The next thing he knew he was waking up and it was almost dark. He got up and walked to the door. Scooter was squatting down outside the door with his weapon trained on the jungle.

Scooter glanced at Josh, put one dirty finger to his lips, and then motioned for him to get down. Josh dropped to his knees. He looked out into the trees where Scooter had his rifle pointing. He didn't see anything. Josh thought maybe Scooter's training and years with the Seal Team helped him.

After fifteen minutes of sitting very still in one position on his knees, Josh tried to move a little. The movement made Scooter's head snap around and he glared at Josh. After another ten minutes, Scooter tapped him on the shoulder. He made the same motion as before. He placed his finger to his lips and then motioned for Josh to move back into the hut.

Josh was relieved. Cautiously, he crawled back into the hut and stood up. Scooter crawled in the door, stood up, and said in a normal voice, "Why don't you get yourself something to eat?"

Josh stood and looked at him in amazement. Outside, Scooter had acted like their lives were in danger, but inside the grass hut, he acted like they were in a soundproof room. Josh didn't know what to think. He went over to the MREs and started to go through them, but then he remembered they were all the same meal. Josh picked one out, opened it, and began to prepare it. Scooter did the same.

Josh got his meal ready and sat on the edge of the cot. He was going to pray, so he glanced over at Scooter who was staring at him again. When Scooter figured out that Josh was going to pray, he frowned and turned his back.

Josh shook his head and closed his eyes. *Father, thank You for this food that You have provided. Thank You that You have chosen this way, at this time, to save me. Please give me the boldness I need to share Your love with Scooter at the right time. In Jesus' name, amen.*

When Josh looked up, Scooter was staring at him again. He didn't say anything, he just sat and looked. After what seemed like an eternity, he finally spoke.

"What did you start to say when I cut you off?" Scooter asked as he looked down.

Josh was stunned. He sat staring back at Scooter. Finally, it came to him.

"The Bible says, 'For God so loved the world that He gave His only begotten Son, that whoever believes in Him should not perish but have everlasting life.'" There. He finally got to say it.

"I had a Sunday school teacher that used to say that verse all the time. Makes you kinda think, doesn't it?" That was all Scooter said.

"Yeah, it does. I think that God…" Scooter held up his hand like a stop sign, and Josh had to stop again. At least he got to tell him the relevant part of the gospel. He wanted to say more to Scooter. He wanted to tell him how much God loves him and that he could be forgiven, but that would have to wait for God's timing.

Thank You, Lord, for Your introduction.

Josh's thoughts were interrupted by Scooter. Scooter dropped his meal in the middle of the hut and grabbed his rifle. He went to the hole in the side of the shelter behind Josh.

The first thing out of his mouth in a whisper was, "Douse the candle." He crawled to the edge of the hut and peered out into the darkness.

"Guatemalans!" he whispered again. That startled Josh. He put down his meal, blew out the candle, and kneeled down on the floor right next to Scooter's dinner.

Josh sat there for ten minutes before he crawled over to the same hole that Scooter was looking through.

"I don't see anything," Josh whispered.

"Wait. You will." Scooter sat a minute. "There! Look over there!"

Josh looked over to the other side of the window. He saw a light moving through the jungle. Then it went out. A little later another one appeared running through the trees, then it disappeared.

"Why do the lights go out?" Josh whispered.

"They're headlamps and they're turning their heads."

Josh sat and watched the lights for a long time. He noticed that they did strange things. They would move along in a straight line and then turn off, or they would walk together on a particular path then suddenly go straight up. Now and then they would even go down. He really couldn't tell how far away they were.

As he sat there watching, a light went right by the hole, turned, went straight up, and then turned off. Fireflies! They weren't Guatemalans. They were fireflies.

Josh didn't know what to do. Should he say something to Scooter? He decided to let him think they were the enemy. Now and then, he heard a loud "click" coming from the old M16. When he turned around and looked at Scooter, he was sighting down the barrel and then another "click."

"Got another one of them!" he whispered.

That scared Josh. A grown man with no ammunition, shooting an empty gun at fireflies, thinking he shot the enemy. Of course, that was better than doing it for real, but it still made him nervous.

The sound of rain on the roof of the hut brought the firefly lights to an end. Scooter put his weapon down, stood up, and hobbled over to the cot.

"Those rascals take all their dead and wounded with them like we do. I've never even found one of them when the sun rises. Why don't you get some sleep and we'll get started in the morning."

Josh could tell that Scooter was tired. All that sitting on the floor the last couple of nights must have gotten to him.

"Why don't you sleep on the cot? I'm going to keep watch tonight," Josh said as he walked over to the hole where Scooter usually watched and sat down. "If I see anything, I'll wake you up."

"Sounds good, marine." Scooter unlaced his boots, slipped them off, and then lay down on the cot. He sighed and then immediately started to snore.

CHAPTER 6

"Get up, marine! We're burning daylight." Josh tried to open his eyes. It was still dark.

"What time is it?" he mumbled.

"4:30 a.m. Time to get some chow and get on the march. We've got to do twenty-five miles today, so let's get going."

Josh tried to act excited, but it was hard in the morning. Especially when he couldn't see anything. He got up off the ground and stretched. He hurt all over. He hadn't slept seated on the ground for a long time. His mouth was dry and tasted nasty.

He walked over to where the food was piled up and grabbed the first package. He mechanically went through all of the steps to prepare the food. While the food was cooking, Josh closed his eyes.

Father, thank You for this day. Thank You for the food that You have provided. Help us find our way to the

Anderson's. Father, give me an opportunity to witness to Scooter today. Open his heart to You and Your love for him. Be with my parents today and give them peace. Somehow, let them know I'm ok. In Jesus' name, amen.

"You must have had a lot to say to the Man Upstairs."

"Yes, I did."

"Did you talk to Him about me?"

"Yeah...yes, I did."

"What did you say?" Scooter asked, putting his hands on his hips.

"Well...I asked Him to let me witness to you today," Josh said in a quiet tone.

Scooter stood staring at Josh.

Josh swallowed, looked down, and thought he might as well go for it.

"Scooter, God loves you so much that He gave His only Son for you to die in your place. And if you believe in Him, you can have eternal life in heaven with Him." There, he said it. Scooter stood there staring at Josh for what seemed like an eternity. Josh got uncomfortable and started to reach for the MRE.

"Let's move out, marine," snapped Scooter.

"I haven't eaten yet!"

"Too late! We're wasting time! Meet me outside in one minute!" Scooter said like he was talking to a recruit and walked outside into the early dawn morning.

Josh grabbed the MRE, pulled out the crackers, and went outside. Scooter was standing down the trail about twenty-five yards and motioned for him to follow. When he saw him come out of the door, he turned and started to jog down the runway. Josh started to run to try and keep up with him.

Josh was having a hard time keeping up. Sometimes he could see Scooter and other times he couldn't. He didn't know how an old man could run so far. He didn't even have time to eat the crackers. Scooter ran up a little hill and disappeared over the top. When Josh got to the top, the trees were all gone and there was a giant plain. The worst thing though…there was no Scooter! Josh stopped running and tried to catch his breath.

He walked out into the clearing and tore open the package of crackers. He started out across the field, searching for Scooter, but he didn't see anything. Slowly, he turned around and looked at the trees in the dark green jungle behind him. He searched it hoping to find a familiar shape or something. No Scooter there either.

Josh walked back up to the tree line and stood in the shade of a large guava tree, wondering what he should do.

"Psst!"

Josh stopped moving and turned around.

"Psst!" This time it was louder.

"Where are you?" Josh said out loud.

"Shh!"

Josh searched the jungle for Scooter. Extremely well camouflaged, Josh saw something flutter. It was tiny and he couldn't tell what it was. He stood very still and watched again. This time he saw it. It was Scooter's eyes blinking. The tiny movement was all he needed.

"Psst!"

Josh slowly moved fifteen feet over into the trees. Scooter had smeared a diagonal stripe of mud across his face.

"What took you so long?" Scooter whispered. Josh looked down embarrassed.

"You can sure jog a long way," Josh finally said.

"That's an old Seal Team habit. We don't have time to walk. We have to get in, get our job done, and get out," said Scooter as he sat gazing across the field. "We have to cross the open space. It's about a mile across. When we get to the other side, we will sit down in the trees and look to see if the Guatemalans spotted us. Got it?"

Josh nodded and Scooter was on his feet jogging across the field before he could even gather his thoughts. Josh jumped up and followed. This time he was able to keep up with Scooter. The fatigue was starting to show on Scooter's face. His pace had slowed down significantly.

When they got to the jungle on the other side of the field, they were walking. Scooter was pale and panting. He stumbled off into the trees beside the trail and lay down on his back.

"Are you all right?"

"I'm…ok," Scooter said. The words were broken up and hard to understand. "I need to rest a minute. I'm not as young as I used to be."

Josh sat down on the ground beside him. *Father, help Scooter. I don't know what is going on with him, but I ask You in Jesus' name to put Your hand on him and keep him healthy. You know that I don't know where we are. Amen.*

They both sat there not saying a word, while Scooter rested on the ground. Josh didn't want to rush him. When he looked over at Scooter, tears were rolling down his cheeks. Josh reached out, put his hand on Scooter's chest, and started to pray. As soon as Josh's hand touched him, Scooter began to talk.

"What was the verse you told me the other day? The one I said my Sunday school used to say all the time."

"For God so loved the world that He gave His only begotten Son, that whoever believes in Him should not perish but have everlasting life," Josh said.

"I believe, but how can He forgive me? All I have done, all my adult life, is do things that Jesus wouldn't like."

"But the next verse is important too! It says, 'God did not send His Son into the world to condemn the world, but that the world through Him might be saved.'"

"I don't know how He could. We have got to get moving," Scooter said as he got up off the ground. He stood for a minute and then slowly started jogging down the trail. Josh sat and watched him go.

He wondered what had just happened. He thought Scooter was about to accept the Lord, but then he knew that it was all in God's perfect timing, not his.

The rain started like a lot of rainstorms in that part of the world. One minute it is not raining, then the next minute the rain is coming down in buckets. Josh got up and started to jog down the trail.

The path was starting to go up a small hill and wind back and forth. He couldn't see Scooter anywhere. He came to the top of the mountain and on the other side the trail split and went three different directions. The ground was muddy and there were no footprints, so Josh stopped jogging.

He thought Scooter had gone off into the trees as he did before. He stood still, waiting for him to call. Nothing! After fifteen minutes of being soaked by the downpour, Josh thought he would give it a try. He felt he should not yell because Scooter thought there were Guatemalans, so he would do what Scooter did before.

"Psst." No response.

"Psst...Scooter," Josh said a little louder than a whisper. Still nothing! He tried that ten times. Scooter was gone!

Josh didn't know what he was going to do. He was soaked to the skin. He could go back, but what good would that do?

"Oh Father, what do I do now? Do I go back? Which trail do I take? Where is Scooter? Father, I want to do what You want me to do...amen."

The rain started to come down harder. It was getting hard to see and hear anything else. Josh decided to sit and wait this one out. He looked for a giant leaf on a tree so he could cover his head. When he found one, he broke it off and bent it. He sat down on the ground in a large puddle and put the bend in the leaf behind his head. He pulled the rest of the leaf over the top and covered his face. That was all the relief he was going to get.

He sat that way for hours, listening to the rain drumming on the leaf. He would drift off to sleep and wake up with a start when a cold raindrop would go down the back of his neck. When he peeked out from under the leaf, it was almost dark. The rain was starting to get to him—the noise, his wet condition, and he was cold. He didn't know if he could make it through the night.

Just when he thought it couldn't get any worse, the lightning started. Bright flashes of light would let him see everything around him every few seconds. The thunder was ear-splitting. He watched as the lightshow moved toward him, striking trees and brush only to have the fire put out by the rain. The storm eventually passed overhead and moved off behind him as it grew faint in the distance. Finally, Josh could drift back to sleep.

Josh felt a sharp jab in his ribs. "Joshua!" a voice said. "Joshua, wake up."

"Dad, is that you?" he said as he opened his eyes to the clear gray dawn.

He felt a hand on his shoulder and uncovered his head. It was Scooter, but something had changed. He was wearing a clean, starched uniform and his weapon was gone. He was talking loud. He looked pale and drawn like he was sick.

"Scooter?" was all Josh could say.

"Joshua, I want you to call me Jon, Jon Banka. I started to think about what you said. How God loves me and would forgive me. When you said that He didn't come to condemn me, but save me, that's what I needed to hear. I asked for forgiveness and God did it! Something changed in me."

"Mr. Banka..."

"Jon! Call me Jon. I have a confession to make to you. Let me get it off my chest. Joshua, I've been lying about everything. My wife died a few years back and I couldn't face it. I have a son named Caleb about your age. How old are you?"

"I'm fifteen."

"Yep, so is he. I left him in Alaska with my mother and came down here to the jungle to avoid people. I was wrong. I'm going to take you to the Anderson's and maybe your dad can take me to the airport. I'm going to try to make it up to Caleb and my mother. They need me."

"Do you feel good enough to walk to the Anderson's compound?" Josh asked.

"Yeah, I'm fine. Joshua, I am sorry for everything I have put you through. Thank you for introducing me to Jesus."

Josh nodded in embarrassment and said, "Which way do we go?"

Jon pointed up one of the trails and started to walk first. He didn't seem to have the drive he had before. Something was different about him. Not only the clean uniform, but something else.

Father, thank You for saving Mr. Banka. Thank You for the change in his life that makes him want to go home, face his past, and be with his son and mother. Give him wisdom as he tries to make things right. Amen.

"Mr....uh, Jon. Does your family know Jesus?" Josh asked.

"The last contact I had with my son was a year and a half ago. He tried to lead me to Jesus. He's a kid a lot like you. My mother saw to that. I praise God for that! I can't wait to tell him I accepted Jesus and He has forgiven..." tears interrupted the rest of Jon's sentence. He stopped and wiped his face and head with a clean handkerchief he pulled from his pocket. Josh walked up beside him and put his hand on his arm.

"Father, thank You for Jon. Thank You, Lord, that You have forgiven his sins and someday Jon, Caleb, his mother, and I will get to be with You in heaven. Bless him richly now. Amen."

"Amen!"

Jon turned and started down the trail without saying another word. He walked about a hundred yards and then stopped. When he turned around and looked at Josh, he had a puzzled expression on his face. He tried to talk, but every word came out muddled.

Josh noticed the right side of Jon's face and mouth were starting to droop. Jon reached up, grabbed his right arm, and then collapsed to the ground as Josh ran to him. Jon tried to speak, but could only mumble. The entire right side of his face now drooped. It looked like he had a stroke, but Josh wasn't sure. He had once caught a glance of someone having a stroke, but then his mother had sent him away.

"Oh Lord, not here, not now!" Josh prayed.

CHAPTER 7

Doug decided to look for his son another way. He couldn't find him by air, so he would try someone on the ground. He wanted to ask if there was an abandoned airstrip anywhere that he had missed.

"Liz, I'm going into town to see General Hernandez to ask him a few questions. Maybe he has an idea where we can find Joshua."

Liz started to talk, but couldn't because of her tears. Doug walked up to her and put his arm around her.

"It will be all right. I have this feeling that Joshua is ok and we will find him. Dear Father in heaven, thank You for this time of testing. Help us be strong and to trust You. Even if You choose to have this work out another way, we know You have a plan that is best for us. We thank You for…" Doug couldn't finish. Finally, all he could get out was, "Help us, Father. Give us strength." He held Liz tightly, turned, and walked out the door.

The drive into town seemed longer than usual. Doug pulled the truck into the Belize Defense Force headquarters and went inside. General Hernandez was standing in the lobby with two soldiers, looking over some papers that the sergeant had given him. When he saw Doug come through the door, he handed the papers back, turned, and walked up to him.

"Doug Powers, praise the Lord! I haven't seen you in a hundred years."

"It has been a long time, general," Doug said.

"What brings you here?"

"My son, Joshua, didn't show up at the Anderson's. He was flying out there to get Jill Anderson and her son to take them to the doctor. We can't find him..." Doug's speech broke up.

"I'm so sorry, Doug! What can I do to help?" the general said, putting his arm around Doug's shoulders.

"I wanted to know if you know of any abandoned airstrips or anything that Joshua might have landed on out in the jungle?"

General Hernandez thought for a long time. "There is a strip that we started to build out in sector seven, but we abandoned it a few years back. That's the only one between you and the Anderson's place."

"I think I flew over that one and didn't see anything," Doug said.

"I'll send Sergeant Gonzalez and a couple of men out there to look the airfield over. It is close to the Guatemalan border. We need to send a patrol out there anyway…as soon as I can find a vehicle."

"I'll drive them out myself. I have to look. We'll stop and tell Liz on the way."

General Hernandez put his hand on Doug's shoulder. "Father in heaven," he prayed, "thank You for Doug and Liz's testimony, and their faithfulness to You and Your word. Without them You know I would be lost and going to hell. Father, give them peace as they look for their son, Joshua. Protect that boy. Reunite them all. In Jesus' precious name, I pray, amen."

"Thank you," Doug whispered.

"Sergeant!" the general bellowed. Sergeant Gonzalez came trotting around the corner.

"Yes, sir!" he said, standing at attention.

"Sergeant, take those other two men, get your weapons and overnight packs, and go with Mr. Powers. Show him where that airfield is that we were building in sector seven. Do you remember where it is?"

"Yes, sir, I do, sir."

"Take a map."

"Yes, sir!" the soldier shouted.

"Meet Mr. Powers out front in ten minutes at his vehicle. Dismissed!" Gonzalez saluted, turned, and jogged back around the corner.

"Thank you, Roberto," Doug said as he shook the general's hand.

"You will find your son," the general said. "I know you will."

Doug waited by his truck for three minutes before the men came out. They threw their gear into the back.

"Sergeant, why don't you ride up front with me," Doug said.

The sergeant nodded and opened the passenger door, sat in the seat, and stood his weapon between his legs. There was an awkward silence at first.

"Why are we going to the airfield?" Sergeant Gonzalez asked.

"We think our son had to land his airplane somewhere between our place and another missionary compound. And we can't find him. I want to look out there to see if I missed anything from the air."

"How old is your son?"

"He's fifteen, but he is a good pilot. He would be able to land an airplane in an emergency if he had a place to land." Sergeant Gonzalez nodded then turned and looked out his window. After ten more minutes of silence without looking at Doug, the sergeant said, "Are you the missionary pilot, Mr. Powers, that the general talks about all the time?"

"I don't know if the general talks about me all the time, but I am Doug Powers. What's your first name, sergeant?"

"Juan, Juan Gonzalez," he said and held out his hand to Doug. They shook hands.

"Well, Juan, has anyone ever told you about Jesus?"

"Not really. I would like to know about Him. I see the general, how happy he is, how he gets along with his wife and kids. He has told us that Jesus changed his life."

"Jesus can change your life too."

"How?" asked Juan.

"The Bible tells us that God loves us and if we turn our lives over to Him and do the things that Jesus wants, someday we can go to heaven and live with Him."

"What about all the sin and bad stuff I have done all my life?"

"The Bible says in Roman 5:8, 'But God demonstrates His own love toward us, in that while we were still sinners, Christ died for us.' All we have to do is ask Him to forgive our sins and repent, which means don't do them anymore."

"If that's what the general did, I want it too."

[85]

"Talk to God and tell Him…" Doug could not finish. Juan looked up toward heaven.

"God, You know the things I've done in my past—the sins. Take them away and forgive me. I repent of them. Fill me with Your love. Change my life. Help me to tell my wife and kids what You have done for me. Amen. Is that ok?"

"That was perfect, Juan. Welcome to the family, brother!" Doug said with a big smile on his face.

After they picked up Liz, Juan's excitement was showing. The smile on his face was contagious.

"One of the things that Jesus asks us to do is to tell other people about Him and to lead them into being His disciples," Doug said.

"I can do that," said Juan. "Let me get in the back and I'll tell those guys about Jesus right now." Doug stopped the truck and Juan jumped in the back. Immediately, he started to talk.

Doug watched him in the rearview mirror for a few seconds. "Praise God! That's a great beginning," he said. He saw one of the men laugh, wave him off, and move to the back of the truck, but the other one listened intently.

Doug drove on for an hour. Juan tapped on the back window and Doug stopped, got out of the truck, and stretched.

"I'm sorry, sir. We missed the spot where we were supposed to stop. It's back down the road about ten minutes. Corporal Jones and I were praying," Juan said.

"Praise God! That's a good reason," Doug smiled.

He jumped back into the cab and turned the truck around. "What are you smiling about?" said Liz.

"Juan just led that guy to the Lord. They were praying so we missed the place where we were supposed to stop. Praise God!"

When they drove back three miles, Juan tapped on the window and Doug pulled the truck onto a wide spot on the side of the road. The three men jumped out of the back and slipped on their packs.

"There is a trail out to the runway. See if you can find any trace of it," Juan ordered the other solders. The two men split up and started to wander around in the brush. Juan came over to Doug and Liz.

"The runway is about a mile and a half from here. If we can find the trail it would make it a lot easier to get out there," he said.

One of the men whistled and raised his hand. "Are you ready?" Juan asked. Doug and Liz both nodded and followed Juan. They walked about a hundred yards until they came to where the soldier who had whistled was standing. There on the ground was a faint trail that wandered off.

"Take the point, corporal," Juan said.

Corporal Jones started down the trail. It didn't take long for the group to get to the end of the runway. Sergeant Gonzalez suggested they spread out across it and walk its length. When they had reached a quarter of the way down, they came to the little trees that were all bent over the same way.

"An airplane landed here," Doug said. Liz put one hand over her mouth. They walked three hundred feet more and saw it.

There in the brush was the left strut, tire, and wheel of an airplane. Doug looked up and followed the bent and broken trees to the burned black hole in the trees.

"Liz, I think you better stay here," said Doug as he hugged his wife. When she saw the burnt hole she gasped and started to cry.

"You men stay out here and look for anything that might identify whose airplane this was. I'm going with Mr. Powers," shouted Juan to the soldiers. Doug and Juan walked quickly over to the hole in the trees and disappeared.

"Boy, this thing is burnt completely! It looks like the type of plane Joshua was flying," Doug said. There were no papers or anything he could use to identify it. The plane had been burned up.

"Sergeant! We found something," one of the men yelled. Doug and Juan jogged over to where the man was standing. There on the ground was a dirt-encrusted piece of fabric. Doug could faintly see one of the numbers or letters on the wadded up piece of material that was half submerged in a dark brown puddle of water.

He walked out into the water and grabbed the fabric. When he pulled it up out of the water, it was longer than he had imagined. Carefully, he untangled it and laid it out on the ground.

"Praise God! He is alive! Joshua is alive!"

Back at the runway, Liz started to laugh and cry tears of joy.

"This is the number off of Joshua's airplane. He put it out here for us to see. The rain must have covered it up," Doug said, laughing.

"Let's search this whole area to see if we can find Joshua or any trace of where he might have gone," Juan said.

Doug ran over to Liz and embraced her. "Thank You, Jesus!" was all Liz could say. The two stood hugging each other for a long time.

After twenty minutes a shrill whistle came from the jungle about two hundred yards away. Juan whistled back and then came over to Doug and Liz.

"One of the men has found something. Do you want to go see what it is?" he asked.

"I'll go," Doug said. They walked over to the dark jungle together without saying a word. Doug knew that Joshua being alive wasn't absolutely certain yet. He would hate to find him injured or worse now.

Juan led Doug down a little trail that came to the hut. Doug went inside and the first thing that caught his attention was the oil-striped towel.

"Joshua was here. That towel was the one we kept in his plane to check the oil. It looks like he was able to get something to eat too. Praise the Lord! I wonder where he is?"

Doug noticed all the MREs and the old M16 without a magazine. The hut was odd, too, with a hole cut in every wall.

"What was this place?" asked Doug.

"I have no idea. It wasn't here when we were building the runway. There were some Navy Seals out here a few years later—maybe they built it," Juan said. "We have to keep the Guatemalan's from getting this weapon and supplies. The border is about one hundred meters from here. Corporal, burn the hut!"

Corporal Jones nodded, took off his pack, pulled out some matches, and lit the palm frond hut on fire. He grabbed his bag and sprinted over to the others as the dry palm fronds went up in flames. The shelter and its contents went up fast, but then settled down because of the wetness of the surrounding trees.

All four men stood there and watched the fire before Doug finally spoke. "Let's get going. We need to get back in the air and start looking for Joshua again."

CHAPTER 8

Josh didn't know what to do. Should he try and go back to the airstrip and hut? But what could he do there? Should he continue down this trail where Jon was taking him? Where did it go? How far was it to the Anderson's compound? He couldn't just leave Jon laying there on the ground. The jaguars would probably find him and hurt him, or worse.

Josh knew one thing he could do. He closed his eyes and put his hand on Jon's chest. "Dear heavenly Father, You know that I don't know what I should do. You know that Jon was helping me get to the Anderson's and now I need to help him."

Josh stopped and looked at Jon. The whole right side of his face drooped and he was unconscious. Josh got up and tried to move him, but he was so heavy. Josh was able to drag him off the trail and under the shade of a tree, but that was all.

"Father, You have seen all that I have tried to do. I need Your help now. Father, give me Your Spirit, help me to know what to do." Josh sat there with his eyes closed and waited. His dad had told him that sometimes you need to listen for God to speak to you. Sometimes you just need to wait on God. Abraham had to wait. Joseph had to wait and Moses too. Josh decided to wait for God to answer.

Josh hoped he wouldn't have to wait the years that those men had to because Jon would die without medical attention. He tried to sit there with his eyes closed, but they kept coming open. He was sitting across from a straight line of little trees about three feet tall. He thought that was odd. It almost looked like someone had planted them. As he sat there watching, an idea came to him.

"Thank You, Lord!" he said as he jumped to his feet. He ran around gathering sticks about the size of the little trees he saw. When he thought he had enough, he came back to Jon and started to pound the sticks into the ground around him. He decided he would make a cage around him to keep animals away from Jon, while he went to get help.

It took Josh an hour to build the cage and cover it with banana leaves for shade. When he was done, he kneeled down and put his hand between two of the sticks, then placed them on Jon's chest.

"Jon, if you can hear me, I am going for help now. I don't know how long I'll be gone. I built a shelter around you and you should be safe." Josh paused and sat there for a moment in silence. "Father...Father, protect Jon from anything bad that might happen. Help me to find someone that can help us. Again, I ask for You to heal him in Jesus' name. Ok, Jon, I'm going."

Josh patted him on the chest and stood up. He didn't know which way to go. If he went back to the place where he crashed, he didn't think anyone would find him. Besides, he wasn't sure how to get there. He decided to continue on the way they were going. At least there was a good path. Someone must use it.

Josh turned and started to jog. The path went from the jungle, into the blazing hot sun of the plains, and then back into the forest. He was starting to get thirsty and he didn't have any water. He came across a small stream that was crystal clear. He was thirsty enough so he decided to take a chance and drink from the stream.

He lay down on the ground and drank his fill. When he was full, he stuck his entire head under the water. The coolness of the water felt good. He took his hand and splashed the cold water over his back. It was almost too cold! Josh walked back onto the trail with water dripping down off his head. He shook his head and looked up the hill. He saw the top half of a man disappear over the top of the hill.

"Wait!" Josh yelled. "Hello, I need help!"

He started to run as fast as he could. The hill was steep and long. When he got to the top, he didn't see the man. Josh stopped and tried to catch his breath. He knew if he waited too long the guy might be gone, but he couldn't run at full speed forever.

Jogging again, Josh went on for a half mile more. When he came around a corner in the jungle, there were two men just sitting and talking. Josh jogged up to them, bent over panting, and put his hands on his knees.

"Are you all right?" one man said as he stood up.

Josh nodded. "I'm Josh…Joshua…Joshua Powers. I…"

"Are you Doug Powers' son?" the man asked.

"Yes," was all Josh could get out.

"I'm Pastor Lopez, one of your dad's first converts over in Belize."

"Nice to meet you. I need your help. I have a man back down the trail that I think had a stroke. He's in bad shape. I'm trying to get him to the Anderson's, so my dad can pick us up and take him to the hospital in Belmopan."

Pastor Lopez spoke to his companion in Mayan and the man got up and ran into the jungle.

"He is going to get some men to carry your friend. What happened to you?"

Josh hadn't thought about the way he looked. His shirt was torn and filthy. His pants were caked with mud and one pant leg was ripped off at the knee. His face and hands were smeared with oil from the towel he had used to cover his head. His forehead, cheek, and chin had caked blood.

"I had a little accident. Can we go back to Jon?"

"Yes," said Pastor Lopez. "What kind of accident?"

Josh started to walk down the trail. "The engine went out on my airplane and I kind of crash landed," Josh said. He was embarrassed and didn't want to look at Pastor Lopez.

"God is good to spare you. People die in airplanes crashing in the jungle. Does your dad know where you are?"

"No. Jon was the only one who knew where I was. I tried to let my dad know, but I'm not sure he ever saw the sign."

"Is this Jon guy a believer?" asked Pastor Lopez.

"He's a new believer. That's what changed him from a guy living in the past, staring at fireflies, to someone wanting to help me. We were on our way to get my dad to take him to the airport so he could go home to his family."

Josh and Pastor Lopez talked and sang songs of praise all the way back to where Josh had left Jon. When they came up over the last rise, Josh saw something moving down by the cage he had built for Jon. The movement made him stop and focus.

When he finally saw the big cat pawing at the side of the cage, Josh started to yell.

"Oh no you don't!" Josh reached down, grabbed a stick, and charged down the hill, screaming at the jaguar. The cat turned and looked at him with a puzzled expression, then slinked off into the jungle. Before it disappeared, it turned to watch one more time.

Josh ran up to the edge of the jungle where the cat had gone, hit some leaves with his stick, then turned back to Jon.

He pulled out some of the sticks by Jon's head and sat down. "How are you doing? Help is on the way, Jon."

When Pastor Lopez got there, he couldn't help but laugh. "Is your middle name, Benaiah? I've never seen anyone attack one of those big cats like that."

"Who's Benaiah?" asked Josh.

"Second Samuel tells the story of Benaiah, who was one of David's mighty men who chased and killed a lion in a pit on a snowy day. I thought I was going to see that again! Well, except for the snow."

Josh was embarrassed. He didn't even think about anything except protecting Jon.

"I'm going to call you Joshua Benaiah from now on," chuckled Pastor Lopez.

Pastor Lopez pulled some of the covering off the top of the cage, then pulled the sticks out of the other side of the cage and sat down. He reached in and put his hand on Jon's shoulder.

"Hello Jon, I'm Pastor Lopez. How are you doing?"

Jon opened his eyes, slowly turned his head to look at Pastor Lopez, and moaned.

"Your friend, Joshua, here, found me and some other men up the trail and asked us to help. The other men are coming with something to carry you. They should be here in a few minutes. I'm going to pray with you while we wait. Is that all right with you?"

Jon nodded his head. That encouraged Josh. When he built the cage and went for help, Jon was utterly unconscious.

"Ok!" said Pastor Lopez. "Let's pray together. All glory to You, heavenly Father. You are the creator of heaven and earth, and our creator as well. You are the doer of miracles and healer of all. Father, we ask in Your Son's precious name to heal Jon in Your time. Thank You for saving Jon. We give You praise and honor and glory. We ask this in Jesus' name, amen."

After a few minutes of silence, Pastor Lopez said, "Joshua Benaiah, you better take that stick and go hit the brush where that cat went. Sometimes they go off a little way and watch you."

Josh was embarrassed, but he got up, grabbed the stick, and walked off into the jungle, yelling, "Here kitty, kitty! Here kitty, kitty!" He was surprised how fast his heart was beating. He had never seen a jaguar in the jungle before

[97]

and he had spent his whole life there. The cat was bigger and more intimidating than he had expected.

When he came back out of the brush, he heard men singing a familiar tune, even if he didn't recognize the words. The men were singing "Amazing Grace" in Mayan, an Indian dialect.

"The men are here," said Pastor Lopez as he patted Jon on the shoulder and stood up. He said something to the men in Mayan and they unrolled the canvas tarp, then they brought it and placed it on the ground. Carefully, they picked Jon up and placed him on the center of the canvas, then all eight of them got around the edges and rolled them up next to Jon. One of the men said something that Josh took for counting, then they all lifted at the same time.

"Are you ready?" said Pastor Lopez to Josh.

"I think we better try giving Jon some water before we go," said Josh. Pastor Lopez said something to one of the men who had a container in a basket around his shoulder. The man nodded and Pastor Lopez took the container off his neck and handed it to Josh.

"He said you probably need a drink too," Pastor Lopez said.

Josh went to Jon and gently lifted his head. The container was made of red earthenware pottery like the Indians had made for hundreds of years. He poured a small amount into Jon's mouth. Some of the water went in and some of it ran down Jon's chin onto his neck.

He repeated this until Jon shook his head. Josh then took a drink of the cold water. It was the best drink he had in days. The coolness of the clear water and the dryness of his throat made him thankful for these men.

He handed the container back to the man. "Thank you! Thank you very much!" he said.

The man smiled and nodded at Josh.

"You guys were thirsty!" said Pastor Lopez. "Are we ready now?"

"Yeah, I was worried about Jon, and I guess I was thirsty too. Let's get going so we can get him to the hospital."

Pastor Lopez said something to the men and they started to walk up the trail. They walked about a hundred feet and then started to sing "Amazing Grace" again. Their voices blended in a beautiful choir. Soon, Pastor Lopez started to sing in English. Josh listened for a while.

"That's beautiful," Josh finally said.

"The whole village is a choir. The missionary who was there before me taught them to sing. They could make an album if they were interested," said Pastor Lopez.

The men sang hymns all the way back to their village. When Josh knew the song, he would join in. He was afraid that his singing wasn't as good, so he sang softly.

When they arrived at the village, the leader of the group of men walked up to Josh and said something in Mayan, then shook his hand, turned, and walked away. Josh stood there with a bewildered look on his face. Pastor Lopez was smiling.

"He said you are a good singer and can sing with them anytime."

Josh laughed. "I didn't think he could hear me," he said.

"Joshua, it's going to be dark in half an hour, so we are going to have to spend the night here. The men are tired. God has kept Jon alive this long."

"Can't we get to the Anderson's tonight? How far is it?" Josh asked.

"I know you want to get to the Anderson's tonight, but it is over twenty-five miles from here, over trails just like the one we came over. Why don't you get some rest, get some food, and we will make a go of it in the morning."

With more than twenty-five miles to go, Josh knew they could not make it tonight. He nodded to Pastor Lopez. "I'll sleep next to Jon to keep an eye on him, if that's ok?" he finally said.

"That would be fine. I'll find out where you are going to sleep and let the people know. You must be tired yourself. You have had a full day," said Pastor Lopez, placing his hand on Josh's shoulder.

"It has been pretty exciting," said Josh. "Thank you for helping me get Jon this far. I don't know what I would have done without you and these kind people. Those men who carried Jon were amazing."

"They say their singing helps them do things like carrying Jon without stopping or resting. I think it is the strength of the Lord. They are good people."

Josh noticed that the people of the village seemed to be heading in one direction. They were all dressed in white. Some of them were carrying a little book. They were all singing a beautiful song too.

"Where are the people going?" asked Josh.

"Oh! It's time for their daily church service. Do you want to go?" asked Pastor Lopez.

"Yeah...yes! I would like that," said Josh.

The two of them walked over to the hut together. Josh was surprised that the shelter was larger than he expected. On the top of it was a cross. It sounded like an amazing choir was inside singing. Josh recognized the tune. He remembered his grandmother on her knees in her vegetable garden, pulling weeds and belting out, "What can wash away my sin? Nothing but the blood of Jesus." Pastor Lopez directed him to sit in the back row.

The church service was a blessing. At times a person would stand and raise their hands in praise. At other times the leader would talk and the whole congregation would listen. The beautiful worship went on for an hour. Then the leader started to speak. He opened his Bible and read the scripture out loud. The people who had been carrying the little book followed along.

Pastor Lopez sat smiling the entire time. Occasionally, he would say, "Praise God!" or "Thank You, Jesus!" Josh was amazed at the service.

"Do they do this every day?" he whispered to Pastor Lopez.

"Every day!" he said with a big smile.

As the evening wore on, Josh could feel himself starting to get sleepy. He drifted off to sleep a couple of times, but caught himself. The next thing he knew, one of the ladies was quietly waking him up. She whispered something to him that he couldn't understand and helped him to his feet. He glanced at Pastor Lopez who nodded, so Josh followed her out the door.

She hooked one arm in his and led him across the compound to the only hut that had a flicker of light coming from it. When they stooped and went inside, there was Jon in the middle of the room with a group of men kneeling around his bed and praying for him.

The men had been praying the whole time the service had been going on. The woman stood with her head bowed until the men stood up, then she showed Josh the old hospital bed where he would sleep, shook his hand, and left.

Josh went to Jon's side and placed his hand on his chest. "How are you doing, old friend?" he said.

Jon's eyes turned to him and he opened his mouth. No sound came out, but a tear rolled down his cheeks.

"Jon, we have to stay here tonight. We will get you to the Anderson's tomorrow. My dad will take you to the hospital. Ok?"

Jon tried to repeat something.

"Father, thank You for these people who believe that You are the healer of all. I ask that You hold Jon in Your hands through the night. Please protect him and give us a safe and speedy trip tomorrow. In Jesus' name, amen."

Josh went around and blew out two of the candles. The third one was by his bed. As he sat down on the bed, he realized this would be the best night's sleep he had since he crash landed. He slipped off his boots and started to lay down.

"Jon, I'm going to be right here. If you need me, try to wake me up. Good night."

Josh leaned over and blew out the candle. The darkness settled in as Josh lay back on the bed. It had a few lumps, but it felt good to be sleeping on something as soft as this.

As Josh lay there thinking about the last few days, he was thankful to be alive. He was grateful that God had spared Jon's life this far. He was also thankful to Pastor Lopez and the Mayan people who helped him. He silently prayed that

God would fully restore Jon and let him get back to his family.

He thought he was still praying, but when he opened his eyes he realized he had been asleep and it was now early morning. He got up and put his hand on Jon's chest to see if he was still breathing. He was.

Josh sat down on the bed, slipped his boots back on, and went out into the gray predawn morning. He stretched and looked around. There in front of him was a faint, partly overgrown runway. Off to the side of the track was a building that looked like it could be a hangar.

Josh started over toward the hangar as soon as he saw it. There was no window in it. He walked all the way around it to see if he could look in. He doubted that there was an airplane, but he wanted to have a look. When he got to the front, there was a tiny slot between the two doors. He leaned up against the door and put his eye up to the crack.

It took a minute for his eyes to adjust to the darkness. There in the dim light of the hangar was the shape of a very dusty Cessna 180. Whose plane was this? Josh was surprised. He leaned forward and looked again. He tried to open the door, but something seemed to hold it closed.

"Father, thank You for this airplane. Thank You that You have provided this way to get Jon to the Anderson's or maybe the hospital. Help me to find out who owns it. Father, You have been so good to me in all of this. Praise You for Your faithfulness. In Jesus' name, amen."

CHAPTER 9

Josh walked in among the palm frond huts to see if anyone was awake. One of the men that had carried Jon was seated in front of his little house. Josh walked up to him, knowing the man wouldn't understand him, but he thought he would try anyway.

"Hi…hello," he said.

The man looked at him and nodded.

"Do you know where Pastor Lopez is?" The man's face let Josh know he didn't understand for sure. "Pastor Lopez?" he tried again.

"Ah, Pastor Lopez. Yes…yes! Come."

The man got up and started to walk toward the edge of the village. When he got to a hut that was separated from the rest of the village, he walked to the front, said something in a loud voice in Mayan, and then squatted down out in front. Josh stood there and waited. Five minutes later, Pastor Lopez walked out and said something to the man in Mayan.

The man stood up and disappeared into the surrounding jungle. Pastor Lopez then turned his attention to Josh.

"What is it, son?"

"Pastor Lopez, I know how we can get Jon to the Anderson's or the hospital in a short amount of time. I found an airplane. It's in the hangar out by the runway. It's pretty dusty from what I can see, but we could…"

"Joshua…Joshua, hold on a minute. That airplane hasn't been in the air in ten years. The gas is bad. The tires might be flat. That is not a good risk."

"I know the battery is dead. We could prop it. I can teach you how. Have you ever started a plane by hand?"

"Yes, I have. Joshua! Have you listened to one thing I've said? I don't think that airplane will fly." However, the only thing that Josh heard was, "Yes, I have."

"When did you start an airplane by hand?" Josh asked.

"A long time ago. In another life."

Josh sat there looking at the ground, not knowing what to say. He knew he should not argue with an adult, but he didn't know if Jon would make the last twenty-five miles to the Anderson's village.

Pastor Lopez walked up to Josh and placed his hand on Josh's shoulder. "Joshua, I was an Airframe and Powerplant Mechanic in the Army during the Vietnam War.

I worked on the O-1 Bird Dog, a Cessna 170, just like that one. Please listen to me."

"What did the O-1 do?" Josh asked.

"It went out ahead of the jets and told them where they needed to bomb. Are you listening to me? Would your dad let you fly that airplane?" he said.

Josh looked at the ground and kicked a rock. "He might if it was an emergency," he said softly. "And this is an emergency."

Pastor Lopez sighed and put one hand on his chin. "Joshua…" There was a long pause that made Josh nervous.

"Whose plane is it?" Josh said, trying to change the subject.

Pastor Lopez looked at Josh and smiled. "The plane used to belong to Henry and Rita Whitmore. They were missionaries here for fifty years. They were friends with your folks."

"What happened to them?" Josh asked.

"When they both died, your folks were on furlough and no one knew what to do with their airplane, so here it sits." There was another long pause in their conversation. "Joshua…Joshua, did you listen to anything I said about the condition of that airplane?"

Josh sat down on the ground, picked up a stick, and started drumming on a rock. "I don't know if Jon can make the twenty-five-mile hike and another two days. God can do a miracle with that airplane and let us fly him there. If Jesus can make a man walk that hadn't walked in thirty-eight years, then He can make an airplane fly that hasn't flown in ten years," Josh said softly as he stopped drumming and stared at the rock.

Pastor Lopez chuckled. "I like your faith, Joshua. If, and I mean it..." there was another long pause. "If we can get all the old gas out of it, and if there is more clean gas to put in, and if we can get it started, and if it runs ok for a while, and if I have the final say on go or no go, then you can fly us out of here. Is that a deal?"

"Oh, thank you, Pastor Lopez!" Josh jumped to his feet and started to hug him, but Pastor Lopez stopped him.

"Joshua! Do we have a deal?" he said. His tone was stern.

"Yes, sir, we have a deal," Josh said.

"I can call this flight off at any time?"

"Yes, sir, you can," he said in a soft voice. Pastor Lopez held out his hand to shake on the agreement. When Josh held out his hand, Pastor Lopez pulled him in for a giant bear hug, then backed off, put his hand on Josh's shoulder, and closed his eyes.

"Thank You, heavenly Father, for Joshua. Thank You that he is a mighty man like Benaiah in attacking that cat and that he has faith like David to say that You can make that airplane fly, just like You made that lame man walk.

[108]

Father, help my unbelief. Father, bring back to my memory all I need to know about the plane. Please help the airplane to run well. Make it a safe flight. Thank You, Father. We give you all the glory and honor. We cannot do this without You and Your ways. In Jesus' name, amen."

Josh stood there not knowing what to do. Pastor Lopez went back into the hut and then came back with a different shirt on.

"Joshua, I'm going to find something to eat, so it is going to be a little while. Why don't you go over to the hangar and see if you can get in? Look the airplane over and be patient."

Josh nodded and turned to go. Quickly, he turned back to Pastor Lopez and said, "Thank you! Thank you for doing this."

"Be patient, Joshua," was all that Pastor Lopez said.

Josh jogged back to the hangar. It was going to be hard to be patient when Jon was so sick and there was an airplane that maybe, maybe could be used to fly them out.

"Father, please let the airplane work. I know it has been sitting for a long time, but You have done greater things than this," he whispered.

When he got back to the hangar, Josh went straight to the front of the building. He searched for the slot between the two doors that he had looked through the first time. When he found it, he stuck his hand in and tried to pull the door open. It didn't budge. He tried it the other way. Nothing! He stood back and looked at the front of the hangar. There was nothing to slide the doors sideways.

Josh walked back to the hangar, bent over, grabbed the center of the door, and pulled up. The giant door started to move with a squeaky, crawling sound. It was heavy and difficult to lift. He had to fight to get it chest high.

Josh got under the big door, placed his back against it, and pushed up as far as he could. Then he turned around and pressed it up like a weightlifter pressing heavy weights. He knew it would have to go up higher, but that was as high as he could reach.

Josh tried to stand outside and let the dust settle, but it was hard to wait.

Be patient! Be patient! he said to himself.

When the dust in the air was mostly gone, he went into the hangar and walked up to the airplane. He ran his hand along the propeller, then walked around to the left side.

I hope the keys are around here somewhere.

Josh opened the door on the pilot's side and looked in. He scanned the instrument panel. There on the left side of the control wheel, sticking out of the ignition switch, were the keys to the plane.

"Thank You, Lord, for this one thing!" he said. "I guess you don't need to worry about someone stealing your airplane out here in the jungle."

The tire on the left side of the plane was as hard as the day it was put on. However, when he walked around the plane, the right tire was half flat. Josh looked around for a compressor or something to inflate the tire. He needed to see if it was going to hold air.

He looked in all of the cupboards for a compressor, but only found a hand tire pump. *What would they run a compressor on anyway?*

"This will do!" he said.

Josh shook the dust off the pump and went back to the tire. He screwed the end of the hose on to the valve stem, stood up, put his foot on the base of the pump, and started to put air in the tire. After twenty minutes of pumping, the tire was full. Now he just needed to wait and see if the tire would hold the air he had pumped in.

With that done, he unscrewed the pump just as Pastor Lopez walked into the hangar. Pastor Lopez grabbed the hangar door and pushed it all the way up. More dust showered down on the plane.

"Man, is this thing dirty! Let's get it out of the hangar. I'm going to get some men and some water to wash it before I do anything to it," said Pastor Lopez.

Josh was covered with dust and sneezed several times.

"I worry about the dust, Joshua. Maybe I should have them bathe you too!"

Josh laughed and sneezed a few more times. He knew a little more dirt couldn't make him look any worse than he already did. The lump and bruise on his face, his shredded shirt, filthy pants with one leg torn off at the knee, and all the scratches that he had acquired—what was a little dust?

"Joshua, get in the cockpit and make sure the parking brake is off," Pastor Lopez said as he walked to the other side of the plane and leaned on the wing strut. Josh crawled up onto the seat and checked the brake.

"The brake is off," he shouted.

"Let's remove the chocks and push this thing out into the sunlight."

Josh jumped out, kicked the chock away from the tire, and grabbed the strut.

"Ready!" he said.

The airplane was lighter than Josh had expected. They rolled the plane outside the hangar. Josh was shocked at how dirty it was. It had ten years of dust and dirt on it. The numbers on the aluminum side were invisible.

"Joshua, we're going to need fresh gasoline. See if you can find any while I am gone. I'm going to get some men to wash the plane."

Josh nodded and walked back into the hangar. In one of the back corners were ten five-gallon cans stacked up. He read the label on one of the cans and it said "cooking oil." He wondered why someone would have cooking oil stored in an airplane hangar. If it were aviation gasoline, it would have water in the bottom of the can.

Josh carefully lifted the can off the stack and set it on the workbench. He tried to loosen the lid, but it was too tight. He went to the toolbox, but couldn't find anything to open the can. He searched the wall of the hangar and found a pipe wrench that opened wide enough. With the wrench he opened the lid on the can. He stuck his finger in the liquid. It wasn't cooking oil. He pulled it out and smelled it. The rich smell of aviation gas invaded his nose. He put the lid back on and found a rag to wipe his hands.

The men showed up with a different container of water and soap. They started to sing "How Great Thou Art" in Mayan as they washed the airplane. They sang in beautiful harmony. Josh wished that he could understand what they were singing. He sang along in English, but he only knew the first verse and chorus, so he repeated that verse.

"Why don't you get in and clean the inside, Joshua," said Pastor Lopez. "It has to be pretty dirty too."

One of the men gave him a little container of water and a wet rag. Josh got in the plane and started to wipe down everything. It didn't take him very long. When he got out of the cockpit, the men were drying the plane. It almost looked brand new. When the men had finished, they walked away, still singing that beautiful song.

Pastor Lopez had gone to the right wing and started to drain all the old gas out of the tank. When that was done, he went to the left wing and drained that tank.

"Did you find any gasoline, Joshua?"

"Yes, I did. There are ten five-gallon cans in the back of the hangar," said Josh.

"You didn't find a large tank, did you?"

"No. I thought that Mr. Whitmore probably had to haul his gas out here in five-gallon cans because there is no road to drive a truck out here to fill a large tank."

"Good thinking! You are probably right. See if you can find the pump that he used to put the gas in the plane," said Pastor Lopez.

Pastor Lopez then opened the cowling on the engine. Something had built a nest on top. The whole compartment was full of sticks and twigs and other things.

"We have a visitor!" he said. "I'll have to clean this all out. It could start a fire if I don't." He went to the other side of the plane and opened that cowling. He went back into the hangar and looked for a tool to scrape all of the nest out of the engine compartment. On the bench, he found a small green garden rake and a brush.

Pastor Lopez scraped everything off the engine and onto the ground, then with the brush he swept the engine clean. He had to get a screwdriver to get some of the sticks out of the cooling fins on the engine.

"Joshua, have you found that pump yet?" he shouted as he was putting the finishing touches on the engine. "We can't pour the gas from those cans because it will put more water back in the tank."

"Yes, sir, I have," he said as he walked out beside Pastor Lopez.

"I have to drain the lower part of this system. You know the line that comes from the tank to the carburetor, all that stuff? We need to get it as clean as we can." Pastor Lopez reached in by the firewall of the airplane and started to drain the lower system.

"If we are careful, we can pump about four gallons out of each can. That way we won't get the water in the bottom of the can. That will give us about...how many cans did you say there were?" asked Pastor Lopez.

"There are ten," said Josh.

"Ah...that will give us about forty gallons. That should be enough gas to get us over to the Anderson's. That is...if we are going."

"Are you going with us?"

Pastor Lopez stopped working, turned, and looked at Josh. "Do you think I would let you go in a dangerous airplane alone? If, and I still mean if we go, I'm going with you." Josh looked down at the ground, embarrassed.

Father, thank You for Pastor Lopez. Thank You that he is the mechanic we need for this job. Bless him and give him the knowledge he needs now to do this job. Thank You that he wants to protect us on this…

"Joshua, would you mind grabbing the ladder and get up on the wing and open the tank? I'll carefully take a can up to the top of the ladder and hold it while you pump the gas in," said Pastor Lopez.

The day had started out with no clouds, but it was starting to look stormy. The sky was turning gray behind them. Josh thought they would be ok flying the other way. He went and found the ladder to put the gas in the airplane, then crawled up and took the filler cap off.

"See this mark I put on the pump?" Pastor Lopez held the pump up and showed it to Josh. "Only stick the can in that far. That way I think we will only get gasoline." He handed the pump up to Josh, who sat down on the top of the wing. Pastor Lopez disappeared into the hangar and came out a minute later with one of the cans of gas.

"Joshua, I'm going to try and hold this can level. It's essential that we do not get any more water in the system," he said.

"Ok," said Josh.

Pastor Lopez took the handle on top of the can and carefully climbed the ladder. When he got to the top, he held it as steady as he could.

"Is that about level, Joshua?"

"Yes, sir, if I hold it," Josh said.

"Let me try and level it, so it sits on its own. You'll need both hands to pump." Pastor Lopez tried to level the can, but it kept tilting back and forth. That went on for fifteen minutes.

Josh picked up the pump and stuck it in the open can. He carefully let it down into the line that he had scratched on the side. Josh then put the rubber hose into the gas tank of the airplane and turned to handle the pump.

"Ok, Joshua, I think we are ready. Let's give it a try!"

Josh started to turn the handle slowly. After a couple of turns, the gas began to flow into the tank. It didn't take long for the pump to start sucking air.

"That's about it," Josh said as he stopped cranking.

Pastor Lopez pulled the pump out of the gas can and looked in it. He was trying to decide if they could get any more gasoline out of that can. When he pulled his head back to think, Josh looked in the opening.

"I think we have about four gallons," Pastor Lopez finally said.

"It looks more like three gallons to me," Josh said.

"It is only twenty miles by trail to the Anderson's village from here. Even if it is thirty gallons, that should be enough to get us there."

Josh nodded as Pastor Lopez patted him on the shoulder. He got down off the ladder and went to get another can of gas. Carefully, he crawled back up the ladder and balanced on the top. He took off the lid and Josh slipped the pump into the can down to the scratch mark. Pastor Lopez balanced the can while Josh turned the crank and put fuel in the plane. They pumped the gas from five cans into one wing.

"Get down and move the ladder to the other side and let's put the last five in the other wing. I'll go get another can or two," said Pastor Lopez.

Josh put the gas cap back and rechecked it, then crawled down and took the ladder to the other wing. He climbed back up the ladder, carefully got on the wing, and removed the gas cap.

Pastor Lopez came out of the hangar carrying two five-gallon cans of gas. As he set them down, he said, "Wow, those things are heavier than I remember, or maybe I was forty or fifty years younger when I last carried them." He looked at Josh and smiled.

They now had a routine so the last five cans went into the other wing in only a few minutes. With that done, Josh screwed the cap back on and climbed down the ladder, folded it up, and carried it back into the hangar.

"Well, Joshua, let's see if we can get this thing started," said Pastor Lopez with a smile on his face as Josh walked out of the hangar. "Joshua, pray for us!"

"Dear Father, You know the work that has gone into this, but we want You to be glorified. If You want us to walk and heal Jon another way, we accept that. If it is Your will for this airplane to start, we give You all the praise and credit. Amen!"

Josh got up into the cockpit and adjusted the seat.

"I'm going to check the oil before we get started," said Pastor Lopez. "It's been sitting for ten years."

He walked to the front of the plane, opened the cowling, and pulled the dipstick. Wiping it between his two fingers, he stuck it back into the engine and then pulled it out again.

"Man, this oil looks great! It looks like it was just changed." He put the dipstick back in the engine and locked down the cowling. Pastor Lopez then walked to the front of the airplane. "Joshua, prime the engine."

Josh turned the primer to unlock it, then pulled it out. He pushed the primer in three times. Then he pushed it in one more time to lock it down. "Engine primed," he called.

"Brakes off, switch off, throttle closed. I'm going to pull the engine through a few times," Pastor Lopez shouted.

"Brakes off, switch off, throttle closed," Josh repeated.

Pastor Lopez stepped up and pulled the propeller through so the engine would turn over. He repeated that several more times. "Brakes on, switch on, throttle open," said Pastor Lopez.

Josh pushed down on the brakes, turned the key to both magnetos, and pushed the throttle in halfway. "Brakes on, switch on, throttle open," he repeated.

"Here it goes!" Pastor Lopez stepped up to the prop, placed his hand on it so his fingers didn't hang over, then raised his leg, pulled down, and stepped away. The propeller made two complete circles, but nothing happened.

They repeated the entire process three more times, but still, nothing happened. On the fourth attempt the engine backfired and belched out a big cloud of white smoke. Pastor Lopez called for the switch to be turned off. When Josh acknowledged, Pastor Lopez stepped up and pulled the prop down horizontal, then called for the switch to be back on. Josh complied.

Pastor Lopez pulled the propeller through one more time and the engine started. It ran rough at first and smoke billowed out. Josh pumped the throttle a few times and the engine came to life. It started to run as if it had only been sitting for a day.

"Praise the Lord!" Josh yelled. Pastor Lopez gave him the thumbs up and walked up next to the cockpit.

"You stay here and warm the airplane up, do the mag check, and check the oil pressure. I'll go get Jon. When we get back, if it is still running, we'll go to the Anderson's."

When Pastor Lopez cleared the plane, Josh ran the engine up to 1500 RPMs. Both magnetos checked out. The oil pressure was holding steady.

Josh barely had time to get everything done when Pastor Lopez showed up with Jon and the men who carried him. One of the men got in the back seat and they passed Jon to him. He buckled Jon in the seat and jumped out. Pastor Lopez got in the front seat and closed the door.

"Father, protect us as we go. Thank You for the airplane! All praise and glory to You, amen."

CHAPTER 10

Josh put the power in and the airplane started to creep along the ground.

"Which way is the wind blowing?" he said to no one.

"I think we have to go to the other end of the runway," said Pastor Lopez. Josh nodded, sped the airplane up, and started to taxi down. The years hadn't been too kind to the airstrip. The plane bounced along, knocking weeds out of the way. Now and then, the propeller would hit a tall bush and shower the plane with green confetti.

When they got to the trees at the end, Josh turned the plane around and looked down the runway.

"This runway looks short," he said.

"It looks like they built some huts on the other end. Can you do a short field takeoff?" asked Pastor Lopez.

"I think I can," he said softly.

"What? Did you say, 'I *think* I can'?" said Pastor Lopez. "I can still call this flight off!"

"I've done a few with my dad."

"Well, can you do one now or not?"

"Yes…yes, I can," Josh said with confidence. He reached up and put the flaps down twenty percent, held the brakes, and then started to run the engine up.

Father, You have brought us this far. Please protect us as we go. Help me get this airplane off the ground and give us a safe trip. Amen.

When the airplane started to shake from the engine, Josh released the brake and the plane started to roll. The tail wheel came off the ground in a few feet and the plane gained speed. The buildings at the end of the runway were getting closer as Josh nervously glanced over at Pastor Lopez. He was gripping the door with both hands with his eyes closed, praying silently.

The building was coming up fast. They were too close for him to stop. Josh pulled back on the wheel and the plane went up a couple of feet, then fell back to the ground. He pulled back again and this time it took to the air. He guided it over two of the huts. When the motion of the airplane smoothed out, Pastor Lopez opened his eyes just in time to see the roof of one of the shelters pass about three feet beneath the tire.

"Wow, that was close!" he shouted. Josh just smiled.

"Where is the Anderson's from here?" said Josh.

"See the two mountains off to the south? They're right on the other side." Josh turned the plane and headed for the pass.

Josh hadn't noticed the weather closing in. The clouds were a lot lower than he had thought. He climbed as high as he could and the tail of the plane felt like it was in the bottom of the clouds. He checked his altimeter and it read 6,500 feet.

"How high is that pass we have to cross?" he asked.

"It's about 6,000 feet. If we can stay right at this altitude we should be ok," said Pastor Lopez, glancing at the altimeter. He was still gripping the door of the cockpit like he was afraid.

"How's Jon doing back there?" Josh said, trying to get Pastor Lopez's mind off flying.

Pastor Lopez turned around and looked into the back seat, then put his hand on Jon's leg.

"How are you doing, Jon? Josh is flying you to the Anderson's village to meet his dad. His dad will then fly you to the hospital in Belmopan." Jon slowly opened his eyes, nodded his head, and tried to say something.

"You hang in there, Jon. We'll be there in a few minutes," said Pastor Lopez. When he turned back around, he said to Josh, "Praise the Lord, Jon tried to say something. I think he is going to make it."

Josh kept checking his altimeter. The clouds above the airplane were getting lower and lower. They weren't too far from the pass, but it didn't look right. He would have to climb a little to clear the mountains, which would then put him in the clouds. He hoped he would have enough visibility to make it through.

The notch between the mountains was coming up fast. The plane was below the mountain pass. Josh gently pulled back on the wheel and started to climb. The windshield flashed in and out of the clouds. He looked out his window to see the ground. When the clouds blanked out the front window, Josh turned all his attention to the side window and the ground.

Pastor Lopez grabbed the top of the dashboard and started to pray out loud. The airplane was getting closer and closer to the ground. Josh's heart started to beat faster.

"Lord, we need Your help. Help me to be calm," he prayed.

After Josh prayed, he noticed the ground fall away. He put the nose of the plane down a little. It went down a hundred feet and came out of the clouds.

"There's the Anderson's runway!" he said relieved. Josh pulled back on the throttle and put the nose of the plane down.

"We made…" Pastor Lopez was interrupted by the engine. The engine backfired and shuddered, making the whole plane shake. Then the engine started to die.

"Not again!" Josh said angrily.

He pushed the throttle all the way in and the engine came back to life, only to die out again when he pulled the throttle out. Josh pumped the throttle again. The engine repeated the same thing.

"Get on the radio and put out a mayday!" Josh yelled.

Pastor Lopez picked up the microphone and started to talk, but they hadn't turned the radio on.

"Pastor Lopez, you better turn the radio on," Josh said as gently as he could, while he was still fighting the engine.

Pastor Lopez nodded, opened his eyes, and turned the radio on. He pushed the button on the mic and immediately started to talk.

"Ah…er…ah," was all he could get out.

"Hold the mic in front of my mouth and push the button, please," Josh said. Pastor Lopez held the mic in front of Josh.

"Mayday, mayday, mayday, this is Josh Powers with two passengers. Approaching the Anderson's runway with engine trouble. Mayday, mayday, mayday." Josh nodded to Pastor Lopez who went back to praying.

"Joshua! Praise God! Glad to hear your voice," his dad said over the radio. "I'm in the air. Which way are you coming in?"

Pastor Lopez held the mic back up to Josh's mouth. "We're coming in from the south. Dad, I'm really having trouble keeping altitude."

"I'm coming out to fly beside you. I can see you now." Josh looked out the windshield and spotted the Caravan coming toward them. Just when his dad got up beside him, the engine quit.

"Oh!" Pastor Lopez yelled and slammed both feet against the rudder pedals. His one hand gabbed the handle over his door and the other his control wheel.

"Pastor Lopez! Pastor Lopez! Let go of the controls!" Josh shouted. Pastor Lopez got a shocked look on his face, then he let off the wheel and moved his feet like he had touched a hot iron.

"Son, you can make the runway from here," came the soft, soothing voice of his father.

"Dad, I'm pretty low. Do I need to use the flaps?"

"No, don't, you need to be able to fly."

The trees were getting closer and closer. Josh could feel himself starting to get tense. He didn't know if they would make it to the runway or not. The only thing he could do was pray.

"Father, You have kept Jon and me alive these last couple of weeks for a reason, and I thank You. I want You to be glorified in all that I do. Whatever happens in the next few minutes is in Your hands. Lead me! Amen."

[127]

Josh pulled up sharply to avoid the trees. He knew he could do that a few times, but sooner or later he would run out of momentum. He did it two more times. There was only one last set of trees until the clearing for the runway.

"We're going to hit those trees! Cover your head!" Josh shouted.

Pastor Lopez put both his arms up in front of his face. Josh watched as the trees came racing up to the front of the plane and then ducked below the dashboard. The plane slammed into the trees with a deafening roar. Leaves, sticks, and branches went flying everywhere. A branch that was one inch in diameter shot through the windshield.

The crashing and scraping sounds reminded Josh of the first crash. The plane jerked, shuddered, and then smoothed out. Josh tried to look out of the shattered and scratched plexiglass windshield. A green slime from the trees made it impossible to see anything.

He looked out the side window and through the scratches he could make out the ground coming up fast. He pulled back on the wheel and stalled the plane a few inches off the ground to make a perfect landing. He headed the plane off the side of the runway and let it roll to a stop.

"Thank You, Lord! Thank You, Lord!" said Pastor Lopez.

Josh bowed his head. "Father, thank You for helping us make it to this airport safely." Pastor Lopez laughed. Josh continued, "Father, help us now get Jon to the hospital. I praise You for all You have done for me. In Jesus' name, amen."

Josh heard the high whining sound and the rush of wind overhead as his dad's Cessna Caravan came in for a landing.

"I'm sorry I laughed, Joshua. We did make it safely, and I do thank God for that," said Pastor Lopez. "You're a good pilot. Praise God!"

Josh opened his door and got out of the plane just as his dad taxied up beside him. The co-pilot's door on his dad's plane was already open and his mother jumped out before the aircraft even came to a complete stop. She ran up to him and put him in a bear hug with tears running down her face.

"Hi, Mom, how are you?"

"Oh, Joshua! We were worried sick. I thought the…" she broke down crying. His dad had shut the airplane down, walked up, and hugged him too.

"Hi, son, it looks like you have been busy for a while. What all happened?"

"Dad, I'll tell you all about it, but first we have to get my friend, Jon, to the hospital. He had a stroke or something."

Vic Anderson had come down to see what was causing all the commotion. He was on the other side of the Cessna 180, talking to Pastor Lopez. Vic opened the door of the plane and reached in to check Jon's pulse. Jon's right hand was still weak and his face was showing the signs of a stroke.

Doug walked around the airplane where the two men were talking and ducked under the strut.

"Vic, Bill! How are you guys doing?" said Doug to his old friends. "What do you think, Vic?"

"He's had a stroke all right, but he seems to be coming out of it. Better get him to the hospital though," Vic said. "Let's get him out of the plane and lay him on the ground."

"Joshua, get up in the plane and help us lift Jon out," said his dad. Josh climbed onto the back seat of the plane and unbuckled Jon as Doug took his legs and pulled him to the door.

"Jon, this is my dad. We are going to put you on his airplane and fly you to the hospital in Belmopan. You'll be there in about an hour," Josh said softly to him.

As Jon slid out the door of the plane, the other two men took hold of the tarp he was laying on. They carefully laid him on the ground as Josh jumped down.

"Before we load him in your plane, let's take him to the chief medical officer," said Vic. "Everyone lay your hands on him." Doug and Liz, Vic, and Pastor Lopez all put their hands on Jon.

"Joshua, since you have been with Jon, do you want to start off our prayer?" said Vic. That made Josh nervous. All these older people who were prayer warriors and him, just a kid. He didn't want to mess up.

"Dear Lord...Father..." he paused for a long time.

"It's ok, son. You can do this," his dad whispered to him.

"Dear Father, I...we praise You for Your mercy that You have shown toward us. We know that we can do nothing to be saved or to be healed, but it is all by Your grace. Father, You are the creator of the universe and You created man. You know what happened to Jon better than we do. Father, for Your glory we ask for him to be healed. Not for ours, but for Yours. We ask You in the name of Jesus and by the power in that name, to please heal Jon. Restore him so he can go back to his family. We give You all the praise and glory. In Jesus' name."

Josh kept his head down while everyone else prayed. He was embarrassed. He glanced at his dad. His dad winked at him with tears rolling down his cheeks and gave him a thumbs up. Josh smiled and closed his eyes. When they were done praying, Vic said, "And all the people said, amen!"

Let's get Jon loaded in the airplane and get going," said Doug.

All the people picked up the tarp that Jon was laying on and carried him to the cargo door of the Caravan. Gently, they lifted him up and set him on the floor of the plane. The four men got in the plane, dragged Jon forward, and got a pillow from a compartment.

"That will do it. I'm going with you. Taxi up near the house and let me tell my wife," Vic said. Josh went to Pastor Lopez and hugged him while his dad closed the cargo door and went around to the pilot's seat.

"Pastor Lopez, thank you for all your help and letting me fly over here. I wouldn't have been able to do any of it without you and those men. Thank you again!" said Josh.

"Praise the Lord! Glad to help. I'm not sure the airplane was a blessing or a curse though," he said with a big belly laugh. "God can use men like you, Joshua. Men who will risk their safety for others." They shook hands, then hugged again.

"Why don't you sit up front with your dad, Joshua? I'll kneel between the seats after takeoff. You can tell us all about what happened to you and how you met Jon," his mother said.

Doug started the plane and taxied up next to Vic and Jill's house. Vic jumped out and ran to the house.

"I'm glad he wants to go," said Doug. "He was a medic during the Gulf War."

"I didn't know that," said Josh.

"God saved him out of some bad situations over there. He doesn't like to talk about it." The cargo door slammed shut and Vic stuck his head in the cockpit.

"Let's get going," he said.

Doug slowly pushed the throttle all in and turned the plane onto the runway. The takeoff roll was smoother than Josh had experienced on his last takeoff. He sat back in the seat and enjoyed someone else flying.

"It's nice to have an airplane that you're sure will make it to your destination," Josh said.

"Ninety-nine percent sure," said his dad with a smile.

Josh spent the rest of the trip telling his parents all that had happened to him over the last couple of weeks. From time to time his mom's eyes would fill with tears as he told parts of his story. He finished telling them everything that had happened just before they got to Belmopan.

Doug radioed ahead and had an ambulance waiting at the airport for Jon by the time they arrived. Then he arranged for one of the local pastors to take all four of them to the hospital.

Josh walked through the door ahead of everyone else and went to the counter and asked to see Jon Banka. Shocked, the receptionist took one look at him and called for a nurse.

"Do you need to see a doctor?" the nurse asked when she saw him. Josh had forgotten the way he looked. He had cuts and bruises on his face. His hair hadn't been combed in days, his clothes were filthy and torn, one leg of his pants

[133]

was missing below the knee, and underneath all the dirt he was sunburned.

"No, I'm all right. I would like to see Jon Banka though," he said sheepishly.

"Joshua, I would like you to get checked out by a doctor," his mom said, taking his hand. "You crashed an airplane! Please let a doctor look at you."

"Mom, let me see Jon first, then I'll see a doctor."

The nurse turned to the receptionist and asked where to find Jon Banka. He was still in the emergency room.

"Let's go down to the emergency room and see Mr. Banka, then I'll find a doctor to check you out," said the nurse. Josh followed her down to the emergency room. She looked in all the rooms until she found Jon with a doctor. The doctor pulled the stethoscope out of his ears and turned to look at them.

"What happened to you?" he asked.

"He was with Mr. Banka and helped bring him in. He wanted to see him before he gets checked out by a doctor," the nurse said.

"Mr. Banka is awake. Go ahead and talk with him, then I will have a look at you," the doctor said.

Josh walked up beside the bed and placed his hand on Jon's shoulder. "How are you doing?" he asked. Jon opened his eyes and looked right at Josh.

"Fine," he whispered. "I thank the Lord for you and what you have done for me. Keep praying for me." Josh took his hand and closed his eyes.

"Father, thank You that You are healing Jon right now. You know his desire to get back to his family in Alaska. Please make that reunion happen. Thank You, Father, for Your love and thank You for Jesus' death and resurrection that saves us. In His name, I pray, amen." When he looked, both the doctor and the nurse had one hand lifted in prayer.

"Praise God, amen!" the doctor said. "Now let me check you out, young man. Sit down on this stool."

Josh sat down on the stool. The doctor stuck the stethoscope in his ears and listened to Josh's heart. He had him breathe in and out.

"What exactly happened to you or is this how young people are dressing today?" the doctor said as he went on with his exam.

Josh told him the whole story. The doctor sat there with his mouth open in amazement. When he was finished, the doctor said, "Well, young man, you have got quite a story to tell your children. Praise God! Tell your parents there is nothing wrong with you that some chicken, beans, and rice won't fix. Nice to have met you." He held out his hand to Josh and left the room.

"Jon, I'm going to go get cleaned up. I will be back to see you in a day or two," Josh said.

"Please call Caleb, my son, and my mother in Haines, Alaska. Tell them everything," Jon said as he closed his eyes. "There's only one Banka in Haines."

"I'll be back soon," Josh said and patted him on the arm. Jon nodded and Josh walked out of the emergency room. His mother and father were waiting for him in the hallway.

"What did the doctor say?" his mother asked.

"He didn't tell me anything about Jon."

"About *you*, Joshua! About you," his mother insisted.

"The doctor said…" he paused to add suspense. "The doctor said…if…I…get some chicken, beans, and rice, I will be fine," Josh said with a smile on his face.

"Oh you!" said his mom as she hugged him tight.

"Mom, Jon wants us to call his…"

"Son, Caleb, and mother, Betty, in Haines, Alaska? Already done! Betty is such a sweetheart. She said Caleb would be on the next flight to Belize City." Josh looked at his mother in confusion.

"How did you know?" he asked.

"Two can play your game," she said with a smile. "No, when you told us the story on the plane, I decided to try and call them in Haines. I figured there couldn't be too many Bankas in Haines, so I would call them all. There was only one Banka family. It's not a very big town. Caleb should be here in a day or two."

Josh smiled. "Let's go home. I'd like to take a shower. It's been a long time."

"I would like you to take a shower too," said his mom, waving her hand in front of her nose. They all laughed and Josh gave his mom a big hug.

Doug flew Josh and Liz back to their compound and then he took Vic Anderson home. It felt good to be home. Josh thanked God for His protection and for saving Jon. When he got out of the shower, his mother had chicken, beans, and rice waiting for him.

"Doctor's orders," she said and put her hand on his shoulder. "Dear Heavenly Father, thank You for saving my son. Thank You that You used him to help save another life. Thank You for Your Son who graciously saved us all and thank You for this food. Amen."

"Amen," Josh whispered. He ate the chicken, rice, and beans like it was his last meal. "Is there any more? Doctor's orders, you know." His mother filled his plate again.

When Josh was finished, he went to the sofa, sat down, and within five minutes was asleep. He didn't remember when, but sometime during the night he stretched out on the cushions and spent the night on the sofa. When he awoke in the morning, his parents were sitting at the table, whispering.

"Can we go see Jon today?" Josh asked as he walked over to the table, yawned, and sat down.

"I think we can," said his dad. "I have to go see General Hernandez anyway."

When they got to the hospital and walked in, the receptionist recognized Josh.

"Wow, you clean up well. I bet you are here to see Jon Banka, aren't you? He is in room 203. Right down that hallway," she said, pointing the way.

Josh led the way down the hall. When they got to room 203, he slowly pushed the door open, not knowing what to expect. There in the room was another young man about Josh's age. He was praying with Jon. Josh turned to his parents and motioned for them to be quiet.

They slipped in the room, stood against the wall, and waited. Josh could not take his eyes off the young man. He was about his age, about his height, and his hair looked similar. They almost looked like brothers.

When he said "amen" and turned, he was embarrassed. "I...I didn't hear you come in. Hi, I'm Caleb, Jon's son. You must be Joshua," he said, extending his hand.

"Nice to meet you, Caleb," Josh said, shaking his hand. "These are my parents, Doug and Liz."

When his parents started to talk to Caleb, Josh went over to Jon. Before he could say anything, Jon started to whisper to him.

"I thank God and you that I am being healed. If you hadn't brought me back, I would not have been able to mend and go home. I love my son. He forgave me and has been praying for me for years." Jon started to cry and couldn't go on. Doug, Liz, and Caleb walked near the bed.

"Dad, Joshua has a cabin in Alaska. They invited us out to it. Do you want to go?" asked Caleb.

Jon nodded.

"Oh, I can't wait to see what God has in store for this next dynamic duo—the new Joshua and Caleb," said Doug.

Everyone laughed.